SECOND CHANCES IN HOLLYWOOD

Private Party

Second Chances in Hollywood

Private Party

MIMI FRANCIS

Published By: 4 Horsemen Publications, Inc.

4 Horsemen Publications, Inc.
PO Box 417
Sylva, NC 28779
4horsemenpublications.com
info@4horsemenpublications.com

Cover by 4 Horsemen Publications, Inc.
Typesetting by Autumn Skye
Edited by Amanda T. Miller

Library of Congress Control Number: 2022931620

Paperback ISBN-13: 978-1-64450-545-8
Hardcover ISBN-13: 979-8-8232-0710-2
Audiobook ISBN-13: 978-1-64450-543-4
Ebook ISBN-13: 978-1-64450-544-1

Dedication

This one is for all my friends who long to follow their dreams. Believe in yourself. Even if the world thinks you can't do it, you can. Never give up. I believe in you.

TABLE OF CONTENTS

Chapter One

HOLLY

Seven a.m. and she was in the kitchen, the aroma of baking bread, muffins, pie, and cake filling the surrounding air. She was two hours into her day and utterly exhausted. Owning one's own business does that to a person.

Once the last pie and a large batch of cupcakes were in the oven, Holly poured herself a cup of coffee and headed for the storeroom. Boxes of unpacked books stared at her, mocking her at the same time they begged to be unpacked. She sighed and perched on the edge of one of the step stools.

I will never catch up.

Holly checked her watch. Two hours until she unlocked the doors and spent twelve hours wondering if today would be the day the business took off. It had been eighteen months since she'd opened The Bookish Bakery, and if she didn't start making money soon, the door to her dream job would close permanently.

The phone in her back pocket chimed, reminding her to test the cupcakes and check the pie. She pushed her worries aside—not easily—and hurried back to the kitchen. Ten minutes later, the pie cooled on the counter and the cupcakes were ready to frost.

Holly refilled her coffee, grabbed a dolly, and went back to the storeroom. She planned to restock the shelves, set up a new romance display by the front door, and put out the baked goods for the day. Zoe wouldn't be in until nine, so Holly would have to do this morning's work by herself. She couldn't afford to hire any other help, so the work fell to her.

Not that she regretted one minute of this venture. She'd gone to college after high school, but nothing caught her interest, and after a year, she dropped out. For the next few years, she jumped from one retail job to another, tried going to school to be a chef, and even attempted to write a book. None of them panned out. When her mother jokingly suggested she open a bookstore-slash-bakery, the idea took hold and wouldn't let go. She secured financing—thanks to her parents co-signing her loan—and opened her shop on Beverly Drive, just south of Rodeo Drive in Beverly Hills. Terrified, nervous, and eager to make good on her parents' investment, Holly struggled to make it work. She kept hoping for that one thing that would put her on the Hollywood elites' radar and make her shop take off. She knew it was going to happen, just not when. So she kept waiting.

By nine, home-baked goods filled the display case, and she had restocked the shelves and answered her emails. All she needed to do was finish the contemporary romance display by the door. Holly stepped away long enough to unlock the door and flip the sign to "Open." Zoe was late, so Holly went back to work on the display. She wanted to get it finished so she could head to the kitchen when Zoe finally came in.

She had just stepped back to admire her finished work when the door flew open, and someone burst through it. They slammed into the romance display, and it toppled to the floor. Startled, Holly let out a strangled scream and stumbled backward. Her back hit the comic book rack and knocked it over. Her coffee flew out of her hand and splashed all over the front of the handsome stranger, staining his white button-down shirt.

"Oh my God, I'm so sorry." Holly grabbed her dust rag, stepped over the fallen books, and dabbed at the coffee stain spreading across his shirt.

Why am I apologizing?

The man grabbed her wrist and held it lightly in his hand. "It's okay. I should apologize to you." His voice was deep, husky, and unbelievably sexy.

Damn right you should apologize.

Holly looked up into a pair of brilliant blue eyes sparkling with laughter, and her ability to speak vanished. She could only stare, her hand and the rag still pressed to the man's muscular chest. She suspected her mouth hung open. He was beautiful—tall, broad shoulders, muscles rippling beneath his too tight shirt, dark brown and perfectly messy hair, adorable dimples, and kissable pink lips.

A tiny gasp left her when she realized who stood in her shop.

Caleb Peters. Television and movie star, Academy Award nominee, Golden Globe winner, and one of Hollywood's most eligible bachelors. He stood in her bookstore, covered in her coffee, his money-making smirk giving her heart palpitations.

"Are you okay?" he asked.

Holly nodded and cleared her throat. "I'm ... uh, I'm sorry. You're ... you're Caleb. Caleb Peters."

Caleb laughed. "I am. I'm sorry I startled you. Here you are, apologizing to me when I'm the one destroying your displays and scaring the shit out of you. I'm such an idiot." He tipped his head to one side, and the smirk changed to an adorable grin. "Hello?"

It wasn't until that moment she realized her hand was still on his chest. She dropped it and stammered another apology. How many times was she going to apologize to this man who had burst into her store, made a colossal mess, and scared the crap out of her? She needed to get a grip. She pushed her hand through her hair. "Sorry."

Another apology. Damn it.

Caleb chuckled. "Yes, we established that. And yes, I am Caleb Peters. And you are?"

She exhaled and sent up a brief prayer that her voice wouldn't shake. "I'm Holly Wright. I own this store. Can I help you find something?"

Caleb gave her a dazzling smile. "I am sorry about bursting through the door. I just..." He pushed a hand through his hair and exhaled. For the first time since he came in, his confident smile slipped, and for a moment, Holly thought she saw the man behind the actor. "I saw a bunch of paparazzi up the street, and I didn't want to run into them. It's been a rough week, and I'm not in the mood for their questions about my recent breakup."

"It's okay. I totally understand." She didn't, as obnoxious photographers never followed her. But she wanted to help. "You can hang out here. I guess that means you're not here to buy a book?"

Caleb laughed and shook his head. "I would have much rather started this conversation differently. Something like, 'Excuse me, miss. Can you help me find a book?'" He cleared his throat, took a hold of the coffee covered front of his shirt with two fingers, and pulled it away from his chest with a grimace. "I don't suppose you have a shirt I could borrow, do you? And maybe someplace I can change?"

Oh my god, why does he have to be so adorable?

He was one of those men who probably looked good no matter what he was doing. She wasn't sure how it was possible, but he was better looking in person than he was in the movies.

"Um, yeah, sure." Holly spun around, looked through the stack of Bookish Bakery t-shirts on the counter, and grabbed one she thought would be his size. "The restroom is back here." She gestured for Caleb to follow her.

He didn't move. Instead, he crossed his arms over his chest and narrowed his eyes. "Where exactly are we going?"

He probably thinks I'm going to lock him in my basement or something.

Holly sighed and shook her head. "I don't have a public restroom. I have a small restroom in the back for employees only. You can use that, or I can take you upstairs to my apartment. Those are your only choices." She didn't have time for an obnoxious, spoiled actor. If he wasn't willing to use the staff bathroom, she'd be happy to push him into the alley and let him fight off the paparazzi back there.

Caleb smirked and chuckled under his breath. "Employee restroom it is. Lead the way."

His presence overwhelmed her in the small narrow hallway. Despite living and working just off Rodeo Drive, she'd never actually met a celebrity. Unfortunately, they didn't just show up in her shop daily.

Holly pushed open the storeroom door and cleared her throat. "The bathroom is through there," she said, pointing to the back of the room. "Just go past the shelves and make a right." She held the t-shirt out to him.

Caleb took it, mumbled his thanks, and followed her directions. He disappeared into the bathroom and closed the door quietly behind him. Holly hesitated for a moment, wondering if she should wait. Then she returned to the front of the store to clean up the mess.

Zoe came through the front door as Holly rounded the corner. Her eyes widened when she saw the mess on the floor. Holly hurried over and asked her to go take care of some paperwork in the office. Zoe gave her an odd look, but she did as Holly asked.

Holly glanced out the front window. Crowds of people wandered up and down the street, but none of them came into her shop. They rarely did. If she could just attract some attention, The Bookish Bakery might make money.

Caleb emerged from the back a few minutes later wearing one of her Bookish Bakery t-shirts with a large cupcake holding a book gracing the front. It looked good on him. He was on his phone, and though she tried not to listen, she heard him arranging for a car to come pick him up. He nodded a few times, mumbled something she couldn't hear, and hung up the phone.

"It's going to be about half an hour. I hope that's okay?"

"Of course." She smiled and prayed she didn't look creepy. "I don't mind if you wait here. It's usually pretty quiet." She took a deep breath and returned to picking up comic books.

"Let me help." Caleb crouched beside her and stacked the books he'd knocked over. "After all, I made the mess."

Holly laughed. "Yes, you did."

Caleb shot a dirty look in her direction, but a smile played at the corner of his lips. She forced herself not to stare.

"So 'The Bookish Bakery,' huh?" he asked after a few minutes. "Does that mean you like books and baking?"

Holly snorted. "Wow, can't fool you, can you?"

Caleb looked around the store, perhaps noticing the display case filled with baked goods for the first time. He laughed and shook his head. "My bad. So did you bake all this stuff yourself?"

She nodded. "I did."

"I'm guessing you like to read, too?"

Holly laughed. "I love to read. I read Little Women when I was ten and after that, I read anything and everything I could find. That book is the reason I love to read. Do you enjoy reading?"

"When I have time?"

"Would you like to try anything? Not only can I recommend the baked goods, but I'm also not bad at recommending books. I bet I can figure out your book type."

"My book type? What's that?"

"Well, I think everyone has a type of book they read more than any others. Their go-to genre. Their book type." Heat rushed to her cheeks. "It's silly."

Caleb gave her a reassuring smile. "It's not silly at all. I kind of like it. What do you think my 'book type' is?"

Holly sat back on her haunches and stared at Caleb. "I bet you like suspense… thrillers. Maybe a good crime novel with a lot of action and adventure, stuff like that."

Caleb laughed. "Nailed it. I'm impressed."

"I could help you find a book if you'd like. I have just about everything. Tell me what you want, and I'll grab it for you." And maybe grab a photo for the store's social media while she was at it. A celebrity endorsement would do wonders for the shop.

"I'm not much of a reader. Well, I was when I was a kid. I always had a book in my hand. But not anymore." He shrugged. "Unless it's a script. Otherwise, I don't have much time to read."

"Seriously? You don't read?"

"I read. I *like* to read. I love to read. Unfortunately, I'm always busy."

Holly sighed. "If you have a book you love, you'll make time."

"It's been so long since I picked out a book that I wouldn't know where to start."

"Let me help. I'll find you a book." Holly stood up, shook her head, and tapped one finger against her lips as she contemplated which book to grab. After a few seconds, she turned and darted down the nearest aisle. She came back a moment later with the first book in the Jack Reacher series in her hand. She grabbed a business card off the counter, jotted her cell number on the back, stuck it in the book, and set it on the counter. "Take this. On the house. Read it and let me know what you think of it."

"I told you: I don't have time to read."

Holly gave him a dirty look. "Just try it, okay?"

Caleb laughed. "Okay, okay." His phone rang, interrupting their conversation. "Will you excuse me a minute?" He stepped behind the bookshelf and muttered quietly into his phone. After a few minutes, he peered around the corner and gave her a sheepish grin.

"Does this place have a back entrance?"

Holly nodded. "There's a service entrance in the alley."

Caleb spoke into the phone again, then he disconnected and tucked it in his pocket. "Can you show me?"

"Sure." She led Caleb down the hallway, past the storeroom, out the door, and emerged in an alley behind the bookstore.

Caleb grabbed her hand and gently squeezed it. "Thanks for letting me hide out in your shop. And for the shirt, the book, and the very normal conversation. I had fun. I owe you one."

A large black SUV rounded the corner and stopped in front of them. An absurdly tall, muscle-bound, tattooed man exited the passenger side of the vehicle. He opened the back door and waited.

"You ready, bro?" he asked.

To Holly's surprise, Caleb kissed her on the cheek, spun around, and disappeared into the SUV. Then he left, leaving her standing alone in the deserted alley.

Chapter Two
CALEB

He was crazy to think he could spend a Saturday morning shopping on Rodeo Drive. Not that he was even on Rodeo; he was a few blocks away on Beverly Drive, close to his hotel. Caleb needed a break, needed to do something normal, and needed to get out of his stuffy hotel room. He chanced it and slipped out of his room with a baseball hat pulled down low and sunglasses on. He avoided Alex by going out the back entrance of the hotel and didn't bother to tell him or Tiny where he was going.

Caleb spent more than an hour wandering up and down the street, in and out of the shops. He was enjoying himself until he stepped outside and spotted a large group of photographers down the street. He twirled around and headed the opposite direction.

He wasn't in the mood to be photographed and torn apart by a bunch of gossip sites. Speculation about his relationship with country singer Anne Marie was already off the charts. Were they breaking up, or weren't they? Were they in love, or weren't they? If the press caught him out shopping without her, it would somehow spin into a tale of abandonment and a lack of caring on his part.

Anne Marie's fans were rabid and amplified any slight toward her into something it wasn't. Intentional or not. They held her up like a goddess while also declaring her to be fragile and in need of protection. Being seen without her would be a betrayal. They would make him out to be the bad guy.

Anne Marie's fans—along with the rest of the world—already thought he was aloof and too reserved for the flamboyant country music star. They wanted an open book who wore his heart on his sleeve. But that wasn't Caleb's personality, at least not the one he showed to the world. People considered the actor Caleb Peters to be reserved and almost cold, a man who kept things close to the chest. Only his close friends and family knew the real Caleb.

He liked it that way. He'd spent years cultivating the persona of the mystery man that women the world over wanted to unravel.

If only Anne Marie's fans and the press knew that his relationship with her was all but over. The only reason they hadn't officially broken up was because of Anne Marie's world tour. Pretending Caleb was her boyfriend was good for business.

Two doors down, he spotted a small bookstore, The Bookish Bakery. From what he could see through the window, there were no patrons inside. He threw open the door and stepped inside. He tripped as he crossed the threshold, and the next thing he knew, he was falling forward into a display of books.

The display crashed to the floor, and a startled blonde in a cupcake t-shirt spilled her coffee all over him. He looked and felt like a fool.

So much for sneaking in unnoticed.

Half a dozen apologies later, Caleb found himself in a bathroom tugging off his coffee-stained shirt and slipping on a too-small purple t-shirt that matched Holly's. He tossed his shirt in the trash can and took his phone out of his pocket. Holly offered to let him hide in the shop, and he planned to take her up on that offer.

Starting his day with a colossal mess, a ruined shirt, and a surprised shop owner was not how he'd wanted things to go. Worse was the phone call to Alex.

"Why are you calling me?" Alex muttered. "What's wrong?"

"I left the hotel—"

"Goddammit, Caleb!" Alex shouted. "We talked about this."

Caleb cringed and pinched the bridge of his nose. "I know. Look, I'm in a store on Beverly Drive called The Bookish Bakery. There are a bunch of paparazzi outside. Can you come and get me?" He strode down the short hall to the front of the store and stepped onto the main floor. Holly sat on the ground, cleaning up the mess he'd made.

Alex sighed so loud Caleb heard it through the phone. "Yeah. What's the name again?"

Caleb repeated the name and the location. He peered out the front window of the shop. He didn't see any photographers nearby.

Hoping to calm Alex down, he said, "It's not too bad right now. I don't think they know I'm in here."

"They'll find out. I'll call you when I'm close. Probably only half an hour. For God's sake, stay put."

"Okay, okay," Caleb reassured him. He disconnected, tucked his phone in his pocket, and turned to Holly.

"It's going to be about half an hour. I hope that's okay?"

Holly had entranced Caleb. She was cute, funny, and interesting. Talking to her was the most normal conversation he'd had in months. It surprised him when she nailed his favorite genre, then she shocked him even more when she offered him a book. He had every intention of letting her know what he thought of it, especially if it meant talking to her again.

She treated him like a normal person, not a celebrity. She didn't ask him for an autograph or a selfie. She didn't even try to snag a picture of him in her store's shirt. Holly treated him like he was a normal guy who happened in her store. He was having so much fun with her that it disappointed him when Alex called to say he was around the corner.

Caleb followed Holly out the back door, all the while wondering if he could somehow draw out his time with her. Unfortunately, they had barely stepped out the door when he saw the big black SUV round the corner. He could already picture his brother's angry face.

As soon as the vehicle stopped and Alex stepped out, Caleb kissed Holly on the cheek and hopped into the back seat, the book she'd given him clutched tightly in one hand. He watched her as they drove away.

"What the hell were you thinking?" Alex snapped. "You know you can't go out alone."

Caleb sighed. "Nobody saw me."

"Then why did I have to come rescue your ass?"

"You didn't rescue me, you drama queen." Caleb rolled his eyes.

Tiny, Caleb's driver and second bodyguard, snorted. Alex glared at him.

"I know you're pissed," Caleb said.

Alex shook his head. "Damn right I'm pissed. You know better, Caleb. Especially after the breakup—"

Caleb cut him off. "I know, Alex. I just needed some air. I needed to get out of that stupid hotel room so I could breathe. It stifled me. I'm sorry. And I asked you to pick me up so the paparazzi *wouldn't* see me. Isn't that better than calling you *after* they've got me cornered?"

Alex sighed. "Yes. Just don't run off again. Jesus, you're harder to keep track of than Chris and Miranda combined."

Caleb laughed, and the tension in the car eased. Finally.

Alex turned to look at him, a huge, deceptively innocent grin on his face. Caleb knew what he was going to ask before the words were out of his mouth.

"So who was the cute girl?"

Caleb chuckled. "She was cute, wasn't she? Her name is Holly. She owns the store."

Alex looked pointedly at his shirt. "The Bookish Bakery?"

He looked down at his shirt and grinned. "Yeah." He held the book up. "She gave me a book, too. She was sweet. I liked her."

"Oh, boy. I recognize that look." Alex laughed.

Caleb tried to look innocent and most likely failed. "What look are you talking about?"

"You're interested in the bookstore owner. You have that I-wonder-if-she'll-go-out-with-me look on your face. It's the same one you had in the tenth grade when you fell head over heels for Patsy Johnson."

Caleb shrugged. "I'd be lying if I said I didn't want to get to know her better."

"You want some advice from your big brother?"

"Not really, but I think I'll get it whether or not I want it." His brother had no qualms about sharing his opinion, especially about Caleb's love life. Caleb reminded himself that Alex was just looking out for him. Not only was it his job as Caleb's bodyguard, but it was apparently his responsibility as Caleb's big brother. And he appreciated it; if it wasn't for Alex, he wouldn't be who he was today.

"Ask her out."

Caleb's mouth fell open, and he gasped loudly. "What did you say? Did my older brother, the most unromantic human being alive, just tell me to ask a woman out? You've been after me to quit dating for years."

Alex chuckled. "I've been asking you to quit dating *actresses* for years."

"Dude, you're *married* to an actress."

"See, I'm not completely hopeless with love. Besides, Miranda isn't like other actresses."

"True," Caleb interjected. "She did fall in love with you."

Alex snorted. "Ha, ha, you're funny. Look, little brother, I don't think you should give up on love. What you need to do is give up on crazy, self-centered celebrities who only think about themselves and their careers. Those women aren't interested in finding love. They're looking for their next career move. If you could find somebody nice and settle down, I'd be happy for you."

Caleb narrowed his eyes and made a show of poking Alex in the arm. "Wow. Am I dreaming, or did you just say something that makes sense?"

"Again, you're funny. Just do me a favor and think about calling that shop owner. What's her name again?"

"Holly."

"Right, Holly. Think about asking her out, okay? It might be good for you."

Caleb flipped open the book in his hand and took out Holly's business card. He stared at her cell number on the back.

"I'll think about it."

Back in his hotel room, bored and with nothing to do, Caleb flipped through the book Holly gave him. He read the first page, then the second, then the third. Before he knew it, he'd read five chapters and was hooked. He dug his phone out of his pocket and snapped some selfies with the book, taking several until he got it just right—book, face, and the shirt all in the photo. He posted it to Instagram, tagged Holly's shop, and captioned it "Rediscovered my love of reading, thanks to my new friend, Holly. Check out her store on S. Beverly Drive, The Bookish Bakery. It's amazing." Then, for good measure, he texted her the photo.

> [Caleb: Hi, Holly! It's Caleb Peters. Thanks for today. Sorry again about the mess. I'm really enjoying the book, too. Thought this photo might be fun for you to post on your shop's social media. Feel free to tag me! @calebpetersofficial]

God, can I sound anymore lame?

Caleb used Holly's business card to hold his place in the book and shoved his phone in his pocket. Then he grabbed a soda from the mini-fridge and stared out the window. He checked his phone every few seconds, hoping for a response from Holly, but it was silent. After fifteen minutes with no answer, he shoved it in his pocket and stared at the white walls.

I wish I was anywhere but here.

Caleb hated being stuck in his hotel room. Every problem imaginable haunted his return to L.A. from Georgia. The house he rented wasn't ready, they delayed filming for his upcoming movie because of a problem with the director, and the paparazzi had been up his ass since his plane landed two weeks ago. He couldn't go anywhere without Alex. He was a prisoner in the presidential suite of the Beverly Hills Wilshire. Why was Alex surprised he'd snuck out?

His phone dinged, and he almost dropped it pulling it out of his pocket. It was Holly.

> [Holly: Thanks for the photo! My employee, Zoe, showed it to me on your social media about two seconds before you sent it. You won't believe this, but I've already had three people come in because they saw the photo on your Instagram! I owe you one!]

Caleb's heart skipped a beat when he read the last line. She owed him one. He grinned to himself.

> [Caleb: Glad to hear it. I guess we'll have to figure out some way to pay each other back.]

He added a winking emoji before he tossed his phone on the table. He immediately picked it up, returned to Instagram, and pulled up The Bookish Bakery. Caleb hit the follow button then perused her profile, smiling when he saw she'd reposted his photo with some heart-eyed emojis. He followed the links in her bio to her shop's website and methodically went through it, page by page. He felt like a stalker, but he was insanely curious about Holly.

The Bookish Bakery had only been open for a short time. It was an interesting premise, a bookshop and bakery in one. Holly seemed to run the place by herself save for one employee. Most of the photos showed an empty store. It had been empty when he went in, too. Caleb couldn't help but wonder if the shop was in trouble.

Hopefully, his post on social media would give the business a boost. Maybe he could try to send some business her way. It was the least he could do after she let him hide out in her store then gave him a free book and shirt. If he could figure out a way to get her some business, it might give him a chance to see her again.

He liked that idea. With a smile on his face and Holly's book in his hand, Caleb stretched out on the couch and settled in to read.

Chapter Three

CALEB

He was on the morning news.

Caleb was only half-awake, gripping a large cup of coffee in one hand, hair standing on end, still in a t-shirt and sweats, when the story came on.

It was a fluff piece, a filler story between the important stories, a small piece about Anne Marie's concert in Nashville. As it progressed, it morphed into a story about Caleb missing his girlfriend's concert so he could go shopping on Rodeo Drive.

He hadn't been as sneaky as he thought; someone got a picture of him. It was from a distance and fuzzy, but it was obviously him ducking into Holly's store. He sighed and scrubbed a hand over his face.

Just as the story wrapped up, his phone went off, a string of text messages sending it vibrating across the table. When he saw it was Anne Marie, he ignored it. She was in damage control mode, probably desperate to let him know she hadn't encouraged the story. Not that he believed that for a minute. Anne Marie was most likely the source.

His girlfriend—ex-girlfriend—had a habit of making him look bad. Anne Marie enjoyed the drama, and she enjoyed playing the put-upon girlfriend, abandoned while he made a movie, ignored at an award show, or forgotten while he shopped in Beverly Hills.

Her career was taking off, and she needed to stay in the spotlight. Dating Caleb helped. Being rebuffed by Caleb helped even more.

Once her fans got a hold of this story, it would explode all over the internet. They would rip him to shreds, becoming more infuriated when he refused to comment. It drove them crazy. People thought his celebrity status gave them the right to know everything about him and what he was thinking every second of every day. He loved acting, but he loathed the crap that came with it.

Caleb sighed and turned off the television. He wasn't in the mood to deal with this. He was due downtown in two hours, and he had to get moving. Anne Marie would have to wait.

"What are we doing here, Paul?" Caleb asked. He slipped into a seat at the large conference table.

His agent, Paul, set a paper cup of coffee in front of him. "I told you. It's a press thing."

"What kind of press thing? My last movie is in post-production. We have three months until that comes out, so I know we're not doing any press for it. And the new movie is still waiting for a director. Any word on that, by the way?"

Paul rolled his eyes. "No. Not yet. But the studio is working on it. This isn't about a movie."

Before he could press his agent for more details, the door opened. Three women and two men strolled through, every one of them grinning at Caleb. He watched them warily. They dropped several stacks of papers on the table and sat in the chairs directly across from him.

"It's nice to meet you, Mr. Peters. I'm Justine Wilber-Cooley," one woman said. "I'm with People Magazine. These are my colleagues." She introduced the others at the table as she laid out paperwork in front of him.

"We are *very* excited to have you here, Mr. Peters," she continued. "We can't wait to get started on your cover."

"I'm sorry," Caleb interjected. "Cover? What cover?"

Ms. Wilber-Cooley looked at Paul. "You didn't tell him?"

Paul smiled and shook his head. "I thought I'd leave that up to you."

Justine laughed. "Well then, I guess congratulations are in order, Mr. Peters." She paused for a moment, her grin widening. "You are People Magazine's Sexiest Man Alive for 2022."

Caleb snorted loudly. "This is a joke, right? I'm not sexy; I'm goofy and awkward. I am not the Sexiest Man Alive." He looked around. "Are my brothers behind this?"

Ms. Wilber-Cooley got an odd, irritated look on her face. "No, no brothers playing a prank. Many people disagree with your assessment, Mr. Peters. In fact, for the first time in several years, the vote was unanimous. You are our only choice."

Caleb sat back in his seat and let it sink in. Sexiest Man Alive.

I can't believe it.

The next hour was a whirlwind of signing paperwork, arranging photo shoots, setting up an in-depth interview, and making plans for the shooting of a short video. His head spun. He did not know so much went into this. The next two months were jam-packed with everything it took to get the magazine to press. Then came the announcement, interviews, parties, and more parties.

At the end of the hour, Justine rose to her feet and shook Caleb's hand. "We're really excited to work with you, Caleb." She was almost out the door when she swung around, her finger tapping against her chin, punctuating every other word as she spoke.

"I almost forgot. We throw a gigantic party for you, obviously. Everyone who is everyone will be there. But it is customary for you to throw your own event to celebrate the debut of the magazine. A kind of pre-party thing to unveil the cover for friends, family, people like that. We're happy to plan it for you, but we've found most celebrities like to take care of those details themselves. We're open to whatever you want to do. Tell us what you need, and we will make it happen." She grinned, wiggled her fingers in a half-assed wave, then disappeared out the door.

Caleb threw himself back in his chair and scrubbed his face with both hands. "What the hell?" he muttered. "Sexiest Man Alive? Really?"

Paul laughed. "Yep." He clapped Caleb on the back. "The exposure is phenomenal. Especially with the new movie coming out right after. This will really get your name out there."

"More than the Golden Globe win or the Academy Award nomination did?"

"Actually, yes. Those are both fabulous accolades for an actor, but this magazine cover will put your face in every store in America. Walmart, Target, grocery stores, convenience stores, and of course, bookstores all over the U.S. This is a tremendous opportunity. Besides, it'll be fun. A big party, your face plastered all over the place, interviews, commercials, all that shit. It'll be great."

Caleb rolled his eyes. "Yeah, great. I can't wait to tell my brothers."

Paul burst out laughing. "Oh, they're gonna *love* this. Can I be there when you tell them?"

Four days after falling into The Bookish Bakery, Caleb couldn't get Holly out of his head. He'd followed the bakery on social media and checked out her website repeatedly. He kept thinking up excuses to call or text her, discarding each one after dissecting it into oblivion.

Caleb laid on the couch, his book on his chest and an arm thrown over his eyes. Alex's voice played on repeat in his head like a nagging spouse.

Ask her out.

Too bad it wasn't that easy.

His phone rang for the fifth time in half an hour. It was Tiara, the woman-and cousin-Caleb had hired to plan his Sexiest Man Alive party. He let it ring through. She kept bugging him to make plans, and he kept avoiding her. He couldn't decide where he wanted to have the stupid party. It had to be perfect, unique, and fun. Maybe if he could get Holly out of his head —

He sat up so abruptly the book fell to the ground and snapped shut. He snatched his phone off the table and dialed Tiara.

She breezed through the door an hour later, a smile on her face, a large Michael Kors tote slung over a shoulder, and her briefcase in her hand. She sat across from him and pulled a laptop from her bag.

"You said you have a place for the party in mind?"

Caleb chuckled. "You don't waste any time, do you? Not even a 'hey cousin, how's it going?' Just dive right in?"

Tiara laughed. "Sorry. It has been a while since I saw you. How are my aunt and uncle?"

"They're doing well. You should come out for dinner sometime, say hi. They'd love to see you."

"Let me know when, and I'll be there. But now, we need to get down to business. From what Paul said, we have little time to get this thing going. I want to get started right away." She narrowed her eyes and pursed her lips. "Okay?"

Caleb nodded. "Yes, ma'am."

"Good. Now, where do you want to have this party?"

Chapter Four

HOLLY

It had been a week since Caleb Peters stumbled through the front door of The Bookish Bakery and crashed into Holly's life. Literally. That moment in time changed everything.

After Caleb posted about her shop on his social media, business boomed. Fifteen minutes after the photo went up, several young girls came in, oohing and ahhing and wanting to know exactly where Caleb stood, if he'd touched anything, and did she have any more of those "super cute cupcake shirts" he wore in the photo. They bought shirts, desserts, and one of them even bought the same book she'd given Caleb.

Awed at the response but sure it wouldn't last, Holly happily served them. She figured that would be it. But it hadn't ended there.

People kept coming in. Some of them—especially the teenage girls—were only there to look around, to be in a place Caleb had been. But others who came in bought a book, or two, or three. Most of them left with pastries, shirts, stickers, bookmarks, or any variety of things. She and Zoe worked non-stop, and for the first time since she opened the shop, she made more money in a week than she spent.

Holly hadn't realized the power Caleb yielded. Knowing he had been in her shop was enough to get people through the door. It was magical. Maybe *he* was magical. While Holly wasn't a fan—she'd always thought he was a jerk, aloof, and stand-offish—he obviously had many people who did like him.

A lot of the women who came in wanted to talk to her about Caleb. What was he like? How did he act? Was he sweet and funny? Or was he deep and mysterious? Was he as attractive in person as he was in his movies and on TV?

They bombarded her with questions until she hid in the kitchen and left Zoe to deal with the customers. It was crazy.

She'd expected Caleb to be a jerk; a lot of articles she'd read and the things she'd seen on television showed he was. She'd kept waiting for him to act like an asshole, but it hadn't happened. Caleb was sweet, down-to-earth, and easy to talk to; he was a normal person. He didn't act like he was a big-shot celebrity. She found herself drawn to Caleb, the cute, funny guy who made a mess in her shop and stayed to help her clean it up.

Holly wondered which Caleb was the real one. Something made her think it was probably the jerk actor. There was no way somebody who garnered that much adoration and accolades wasn't an egotistical ass.

Several times during the week, she considered picking up her phone and texting him, but she stopped herself. Who was she to think she could text someone like Caleb Peters? He wouldn't want to hear from her. She was nothing more than a nobody bookstore owner. His interest in her was fleeting, most likely over by the time the sun set on the Pacific seven days ago. Posting the picture had probably been his way of saying thank you for helping him hide from the paparazzi.

"Holly!"

She emerged from the kitchen and followed the sound of Zoe's voice calling her from the front of the store. A man with a camera stood near the front register, snapping pictures. Holly wiped her hands on her apron and hurried across the room.

"Can I help you?" she asked.

The photographer—if that's what he really was—snapped her picture before he lowered the camera and let it rest against his chest. He held out his hand. "How do you do, ma'am? I'm Brian Drain from TGM."

Holly knew exactly who he was. He'd become infamous after Chris Chandler punched him in the face last year. His so-called website was nothing but garbage and smear pieces. It was doubtful his intentions in her shop were anything other than nefarious.

"TGM? The Gossip Monger?"

"Yes, ma'am. Rumor has it Caleb Peters hid in your store last week. It would be fantastic if I could get a quote for an article I'm doing about Mr. Peters."

"I can't imagine why you would want a quote from me."

"Like I said, there is a rumor Mr. Peters was in your store last week. I wanted to know what he was doing here. He was supposed to be in Nashville—"

Holly cut him off, her hand up and in his face. "If you have a question about Caleb Peters, ask him. Now, if you'll excuse me, I have work to do." She smiled, spun around, and quickly returned to the kitchen.

She exhaled and put her head in her hands.

She didn't have time to answer stupid questions about the celebrity who hid in her store for an hour. It wasn't like they were dating or something.

The Gossip Monger could find someone else to exploit.

Her cell phone rang at 8:45 a.m., fifteen minutes before the store opened. Without looking at the number, she answered it, balancing her phone between her shoulder and her ear so she could carry the last pie and tray of cookies to the display case in the café area.

"Hello?"

"Holly?"

"Speaking. Who is this?"

"Hi, um … it's Caleb, Caleb Peters. I was wondering if you had a few minutes to talk?"

What the hell does he want?

"Sure. But can you call me back in like five minutes? I've got a bunch of stuff I'm trying to put in the display case—"

He cut her off. "I'm in the alley. I hoped I could come in and talk to you in person. If that's okay with you?"

"Fine. Give me a couple of minutes, and I'll be right there." She set the cookies down, let the phone fall into her hand, and disconnected the call. She shoved it in her apron.

How presumptuous of him to just show up out of the blue and expect her to drop everything to talk to him. Typical spoiled actor nonsense. He was a jerk.

Holly put the rest of the goodies in the display case, intentionally taking her time so Caleb would have to wait. She catered to no one's demands, especially those of a stuck-up actor insisting on talking to her in person.

She put everything away and made her way to the back door. She unlocked it and pushed it open.

Caleb came in like a man on a mission, followed by a beautiful gray-haired woman and the muscle-bound, tattooed guy who'd been in the SUV the other day. Caleb wore sunglasses, a hat pulled down low over his eyes, a black leather jacket, jeans, and a plain white t-shirt. Holly's breath caught in her throat.

Dammit, don't let him get under your skin.

She pushed a hand through her hair, adjusted her apron, then promptly chastised herself for caring what Caleb thought. She took a deep breath and put a smile on her face.

"Caleb, hi." She stopped in front of him, wondering if she had flour on her face. Out of the corner of her eye, she saw Zoe stop dead in the hall, her mouth hanging open.

"Zoe," she hissed. "Can you go open the store, please?"

"Sorry," Zoe mumbled. She smiled and waved at Caleb before hurrying down the hall.

"I'm sorry to bother you like this, but I wanted to talk to you in private," Caleb said.

"Um, yeah, okay. Why don't we step back into the storage room?" She gestured for them to follow her and led them down the hall passed the rest room where Caleb had changed his clothes.

"Okay, here we are," she said as they stepped in. The muscular, tattooed guy stayed outside the room by the door.

Caleb smiled. "This is Tiara, by the way. She's my cousin and one of the best party planners in Los Angeles."

Confused, Holly smiled warily and shook the woman's hand before she turned back to Caleb. "Party planner? What's going on?"

"I'm here to talk to you about renting your shop for a party."

"I'm sorry, what?" She must have misheard him.

"I want to rent your shop for a party I'm having in two months. I'd like you to cater it as well if you think you can handle it."

"A party? Here? Why?"

Caleb exhaled. "I want to have it here. This place is interesting and unique. I don't want to have my party at some boring venue that's been used a hundred times. And I thought it might be a boost to your business—"

Holly shook her head. "You don't have to do that."

"I want to. And I'm serious. This is a great place. Tiara has some ideas."

"I checked the store out online," Tiara interjected. "It's a great place. I think it has an amazing layout, perfect for a small, intimate party. We would handle everything—publicity, staffing the night of the party, decorating, alcohol, all of it. Caleb wants you to bake though. I understand you're good at it?"

Holly nodded. "I... I guess so."

"Great," Tiara continued. "It will an amazing party. I can't wait to get started."

Holly held up her hand. "Wait a minute. I haven't agreed to anything yet."

Caleb stepped closer, took her hand, and lowered his voice. "Please say yes."

Caleb's deep, sexy voice made her quiver in all the right places. Holly choked back a moan and forced herself to concentrate on the words coming out of his mouth rather than the perfection of his voice. No matter how hard she resisted him, he kept getting under her skin.

"Holly, please?"

How can I say no?

She gnawed on her lower lip. Allowing Caleb to use her shop would certainly help with business. His photo on social media made a tremendous impact. She could only imagine what a party would do.

I'd be crazy to say no.

It took her two seconds to decide. "Yes. Sure. You can use my shop."

Tiara grinned, pulled a bundle of papers out of her bag, and held them out. "I'll need you to go over this paperwork and sign it. It includes a non-disclosure agreement that is not negotiable. Everything needs to be signed if we're going to work with you. I'll be back the day after tomorrow to pick it up. We can go over any questions you have and talk about our needs and expectations versus your needs and expectations. We'll also talk about money. Your budget versus Caleb's budget. Does that sound good?"

Holly took the paperwork with a shaking hand. This could change her entire world, her *universe*. Her whole life. "S-sure," she stammered. "Come by any time. I'm always here."

"Great. I'll see you in a day or two." Tiara gave Caleb a smile and tipped her head to one side. "Ready, Caleb?"

"Can you give me a minute, please? I'll be right out."

"Sure. I'll go look around the shop, get the lay of the land, so to speak," Tiara said. "It was nice to meet you, Holly." She stepped out of the storage room.

"Thank you, Holly," Caleb said once the door swung closed behind Tiara.

Holly laughed. "*I* should thank *you*. This could change my life."

Caleb shrugged. "It's the least I could do. I owed you for letting me hide from the paparazzi."

"You don't owe me anything. Your picture on social media already helped." She held the papers up and shook them in his face. "This is above and beyond anything I expected."

"I love your store. I think it's an amazing place that deserves more recognition. Hopefully, this helps."

"It will. Thank you."

"Can I ask you another favor?"

Holly giggled. "I suppose so. But you might reach your limit."

"Will you let me take you to dinner? As a thank you for letting me use this place for my party?"

The invitation shocked her. Dinner with a movie star. While she appreciated his enthusiasm and his apparent need to thank her for the use of her shop, a dinner date was something else entirely.

"I... I don't know, Caleb. Don't you... don't you have a girlfriend? A pop star or something like that? I thought I saw something online about you and her?"

Caleb sighed. "I *was* dating a country music singer, but we broke up three or four weeks ago."

"Really?" She wasn't interested in the press turning her into the other woman.

"Yes, Holly, really. I do not have a girlfriend. I wouldn't ask you out if I did. I'm not that kind of guy."

She believed him. She wasn't sure why, but his adamant denial rang true to her.

"Please say yes," Caleb repeated his words from a second ago. "It's just dinner. Nothing more, I promise. I want to thank you properly. Standing in your storage room saying it doesn't mean quite the same thing as a nice dinner."

Holly's heart jumped into her throat, and her brain shut down. She blankly stared at Caleb.

"Holly?"

"Um..."

"Are you okay?"

She closed her eyes and exhaled slowly. "Sorry. I'm a bit ... speechless. You keep surprising me, saying stuff I don't expect to come out of your mouth. It throws me out of whack. You're not fitting the mold."

Caleb laughed, a deep, throaty noise that rocked her to her core. He moved closer, so close she could feel his breath against her cheek. "I don't fit the mold. I'm not who you think I am, Holly. I'm a normal, everyday guy who would like to take you to dinner."

Holly opened her eyes and nodded. "I'd love to go to dinner with you."

Chapter Five
CALEB

Half the battle was asking Holly out. It had been a long time since asking a woman on a date made him nervous, but Holly made his hands shake and his stomach twist in knots.

Caleb hated to remind her he was just another normal guy asking a pretty girl out on a date, but like most women, she couldn't get past his celebrity status. He liked Holly, and he wanted her to like him. Her response—open mouthed silence—had convinced him she was going to say no. Playing it off to say thank you for her help seemed to work. It took a lot of self-control not to shout "yes" when she agreed to go to dinner with him.

The difficulty a simple dinner date presented didn't occur to him until he was back in the penthouse at the Wilshire. Anywhere they went presented a problem; the paparazzi sat outside the hotel waiting for him to make a move. They followed him wherever he went, which meant Caleb couldn't go anywhere without Alex or Tiny. But scary bodyguards didn't make great dinner companions.

There was only one place they could go where he might get some modicum of privacy. His dad's best friend owned a small Italian restaurant in Calabasas, nothing fancy, but the food was great. It wasn't anyplace trendy or happening, off the beaten path. And so, he hoped, it was private. He would call Uncle Joe, his dad's friend, tomorrow and see if he could get him a table.

As much as he hated to do it, Holly would have to meet him at the restaurant after Alex dropped Caleb off in the alley. None of this was ideal, but he wanted that dinner with Holly. He wanted the chance to get to know her, and this was the only way.

Plan in place—in his head, anyway—he reached for his phone to call Alex. It all had to be cleared through his pain-in-the-butt brother-slash-bodyguard. Once Alex gave the okay, Caleb would feel a lot better.

Caleb shifted in the booth, his knees hitting the bottom of the table. The vinyl under his ass squeaked as he moved. He suppressed a groan. Maybe this was a mistake. The location, not the date. It wasn't like he couldn't afford some high-priced, trendy restaurant. Except there, he'd have to be Caleb Peters, movie star. Here, he could just be Caleb.

He looked around the restaurant. It was small and clean but dated. The booths had vinyl seats and Formica tabletops covered with red and white checkered tablecloths. Pictures of old celebrities like Frank Sinatra and Dean Martin hung on the wall. The wait staff wore white shirts, black pants, and red aprons. The smell of good Italian cooking filled the air.

He came here often. No one bothered him, or stared at him, or snuck pictures of him, and rarely did anyone ask him for an autograph while he was in the middle of shoveling food into his mouth. He wanted to impress Holly, but maybe this wasn't the place to do it.

This date was different. He needed it to be different. It wasn't for press coverage, and it wasn't at the behest of the studio, his agent, or his publicist. This date was with a woman he liked. He wanted to keep her out of the eye of the press, keep her safe, keep her to himself.

Holly was different.

The bell over the door gave a cheery tingle. He peered around the wall next to the booth. Holly stood at the hostess stand, speaking to Maria, Uncle Joe's wife. She wore a simple, knee-length white and blue dress with matching shoes. Her honey-blonde hair hung in soft waves around her face.

She's gorgeous.

Caleb slid out of the booth and raised his hand to get her attention. A tentative smile spread across her face when her eyes met his. She nodded at Maria, pointing at him. Maria smiled and gestured for Holly to follow her through the restaurant to his side.

"Thank you, Aunt Maria," he said. He turned to Holly. "You look beautiful."

Holly blushed, her eyes downcast, and her hair fell over her face. "Thank you," she mumbled shakily.

Caleb took her hand to guide Holly to her seat. He eased in across from her and folded his hands on the table.

"Thank you for meeting me here. I'm sorry I couldn't pick you up."

"It's okay," she said. "Ever since you were in the store last time, the press has been outside almost every day. If you had come and picked me up, someone would have seen you."

Their server appeared, menus in hand. "Caleb," she said. "Long time, no see."

"Lucille," he replied. "How are you?"

Lucille shrugged. "Busy. School and work keep me on my toes."

"You're still going to school? What's it been? Fifteen years?" He poked her in the arm. "Aren't you ever going to finish?"

"You're funny for somebody who didn't even attempt to go to college." Lucille looked at Holly and winked. "This one thinks he's a comedian instead of an actor." She held out her hand. "I'm Lucille. Lou for short. In case you're curious, I've known Caleb for ages, all the way back to diapers. As you can probably tell, I'm not impressed with his movie star status."

Holly giggled and shook Lou's hand. "I'm Holly. Nice to meet you." Then she leaned close and whispered, "I'm not that impressed either."

Lou burst out laughing. "I like her, Caleb."

Caleb shook his head. "You're ganging up on me already? I can't win."

"You're a big boy. You can handle it." Lou put their menus on the table and pulled a notebook from her pocket. "Can I get you guys something to drink?"

They gave Lou their orders, and she promised to return shortly.

"How does Lou know you?" Holly asked as soon as they were alone.

Caleb grinned. "We grew up together. Joe, her father, is my dad's best friend, and he owns this restaurant. We had family dinners here several times a week, and they came to our place for barbecues and stuff. We've been friends forever. So, when I come in here, they treat me like a normal person, not some hotshot celebrity."

Holly giggled. "I bet that's refreshing."

Caleb sighed and nodded. "I love it. It's nice to come someplace where they treat me like I'm just Caleb. No special treatment, no fawning over me, just an excellent dinner with good company."

Holly rolled her eyes. "Funny. I thought you enjoyed being fawned over. You probably thrive off people paying attention to you and giving you what you want. I mean, you're always in the headlines, front and center, on numerous websites."

Caleb grunted and shook his head. "That's, uh, harsh."

She crossed her eyes and scratched the tip of her nose. She exhaled loudly before she spoke. "Wait a minute. That ... that came out wrong. I mean, I always assumed *all* actors like to be fawned over and have everyone pay attention to them. Isn't that why you became an actor? Because you want everyone to look at you?"

Caleb furrowed his brows. It never occurred to him that people thought he was an actor because he liked the attention.

"I never thought of it like that. I enjoy acting. I enjoy pretending to be someone I'm not. I enjoy the challenge of creating a new persona out of nothing. I didn't get into this business because I want people to look at me or *fawn* over me, as you say. I genuinely like what I do. I love what I do."

He thought Holly might have had something more to say, but Lou appeared with their drinks—white wine for her, and an iced tea for him.

"I didn't look at the menu," Holly mumbled.

"I know what's good," Caleb said. "How about I order for us?"

"That sounds great." She wouldn't look at him or talk to him. He had upset her. Things were off to a terrible start.

Flustered, Caleb quickly gave Lou their orders and handed her the menus. "Thanks, Lou."

"No problem," she replied. "Dad says hi, by the way. You should stop by the kitchen before you leave."

He nodded. "I'll try."

Lou squeezed Caleb's arm. "Try hard." She spun on her heel and headed for the kitchen.

"I didn't mean to offend you," Holly whispered as soon as Lou was out of earshot.

"I wasn't offended." He reached across the table and grabbed Holly's hand, squeezing it gently.

Holly made a face. "Yeah right. I basically implied you enjoy being the center of attention and sucking up all the glory—"

"That's not what I thought you meant," he interrupted. "Not at all." Except he did think she meant it, and it hurt his feelings. He wanted Holly to like him, not think he was some asshole celebrity who demanded attention all the time.

She exhaled and shook her head. She pulled her hands free, folded them in her lap, and stared at them. "I'm in over my head."

"What do you mean?" He sipped his iced tea.

"You. I'm in over my head with you. You're a big movie star. God, Caleb, you're *the* movie star. Everybody knows you, and everyone loves you. Me? I'm a nobody. I own a struggling bookstore off Rodeo Drive that no one has heard of. Nobody knows me or cares about me." She chuckled, the sound far from joyous or humorous. "I shouldn't be here." She picked up her purse and slid to the edge of the booth. "I'm going to go."

Caleb jumped to his feet and stepped in front of her. "Please don't. Please ... just ... have one dinner with me. Give me a chance."

For a single heartbeat, Caleb thought she would leave and his only chance to impress this woman, to get her to see him as more than Caleb the actor, would leave with her. He silently pleaded with whatever God looked out for actors to give him this one thing.

Holly sighed and tossed her purse onto the seat. "Okay, I'll stay. For a little while."

Caleb grinned. "Thank you. You won't regret it."

Chapter Six

HOLLY

I'm in over my head.

Holly repeated that statement over and over in her head all the way to the restaurant. Caleb picked the place, a family-owned restaurant in Calabasas. He told her it had been around for thirty years—Marino's Italian Restaurant—and it was one of his favorites. She was supposed to give her name when she arrived; they would know why she was there.

The only reason she'd agreed to dinner with Caleb was because of the party. She considered canceling until she read through the paperwork and saw the exorbitant amount of money they offered her. She would do whatever she could to make this party a success. It meant big things for her shop—publicity, recognition, and an influx of cash to get her back on her feet. If she had to sit through dinner with an obnoxious, stuck-up celebrity, so be it.

She found the restaurant easily enough, thanks to her knowledgeable Uber driver. It wasn't at all what she'd expected—small, almost intimate, and off the beaten path. No paparazzi or press stood outside the door, and she didn't see Caleb's big, black SUV or his bodyguards anywhere.

When she opened the door, a little bell jingled pleasantly, and the woman at the hostess stand gave her a sweet smile. The smile widened when she said her name. She gestured for Holly to follow her.

Caleb stood beside a table in the back. He thanked the hostess—Aunt Maria?—and took Holly's hand. Her stomach flipped, and her heart raced, a reaction she hadn't expected. It would be hard to enjoy herself if her stomach didn't stop twisting.

I'm in over my head. She exhaled. *This is just a thank you dinner. That's all.*

Her self-reassurances did nothing to quell her nerves. She eased into the booth across from Caleb and clutched her hands in her lap, where he couldn't see them. She resisted the urge to pinch herself.

This can't be real; I can't be sitting at a table with Caleb Peters.

She was nothing, a nobody, and not sure what she was doing on a date with Caleb Peters. He should be with someone famous like him.

"Thank you for meeting me here. I'm sorry I couldn't pick you up," he said.

"It's okay," Holly replied. She would never admit it had annoyed her when he called and asked her to meet him at the restaurant. Another hint that this wasn't a conventional date. "Ever since you were in the store, the press has been outside almost every day. If you had come and picked me up, someone would have seen you." That was what she'd been telling herself, anyway.

Their server appeared, menus in hand. "Caleb," she said. "Long time, no see."

Caleb blatantly flirted with the waitress. It irked Holly, but she did her best not to react. The relief that flooded her when Lou introduced herself was like a bothersome mosquito being squashed. She bit her tongue so she didn't blurt out, "Oh, you're an old friend!"

It shouldn't bother her that Caleb flirted with anyone. This was nothing more than a thank you dinner. She held no claim to him. He could flirt with anyone he wanted to; it was none of her business.

Holly loved the fact that Lou didn't take Caleb too seriously and treated him like he was a normal person. When she'd accepted this dinner invitation, she thought she'd have to deal with people falling over themselves to impress Caleb all night. So far, she had seen no one treat him like a celebrity. It dispelled her nerves somewhat.

It didn't last. She had to open her mouth and stick her foot in it. The food wasn't even on the table before she made a fool of herself and insulted him.

After insinuating Caleb was an attention whore, she barely heard a word he said. The buzzing in her ears was too loud. His brow furrowed, and his mouth twisted in what she believed was irritation. Not that she could say for sure. Holly forced herself to focus and caught the last of what he said.

"I didn't get into this business because I want people to look at me or *fawn* over me, as you say. I genuinely like what I do. I love what I do."

She wanted to apologize, but Lou came back with their drinks and to get their food order. Holly hadn't even looked at the menu.

She said as much, so Caleb ordered for them. She gnawed on her lower lip as he talked with Lou, wondering how she could make it up to him. Caleb's party meant a lot to her. It could pull her struggling store out of the red. The last thing she wanted to do was alienate him. She needed to set things right. If she could.

She waited until Lou couldn't hear them before she spoke.

"I didn't mean to offend you."

Caleb grabbed Holly's hand and squeezed it. "I wasn't offended."

She frowned. "Yeah right. I basically implied you enjoy being the center of attention and sucking up all the glory—"

"I didn't think that. Not at all."

Her lungs were going to explode. She exhaled and shook her head. She pulled her hands out of his, folded them in her lap, and stared at them. "I'm in over my head."

"What do you mean?"

"You. I'm in over my head with you. You're a big movie star. God, Caleb, you're *the* movie star. Everybody knows you, and everyone loves you. But me? I'm a nobody. I own a struggling bookstore off Rodeo Drive no one has heard of. Nobody knows me or cares about me." She laughed, but nothing about this was humorous. "I shouldn't be here." She snatched her purse off the seat beside her and slid to the edge of the booth. "I'm going to go."

Caleb jumped to his feet and stepped in front of her. "Please don't. Please ... just ... have one dinner with me. Give me a chance."

Holly shook her head. Her gorge rose, and her hands were clammy. But the look on his face was so sincere and honest, it made her want to give him a chance. She sighed and tossed her purse back on the seat.

"Okay, I'll stay. For a little while."

Caleb grinned. "Thank you. You won't regret it."

Holly sat down, grabbed her glass of white wine, and took a huge swallow. She coughed, her hand to her chest, and squeezed her eyes closed. When she opened them a few seconds later, Caleb stared at her with concern etched in the lines of his face.

"You okay?"

She took another drink of her wine, set the empty glass down, signaled Lou, and asked for another. Before she knew it, she'd gulped down the second glass of wine and her head spun. She wasn't normally a drinker—unless it was coffee—so slamming two glasses of wine in less than ten minutes wasn't a good idea.

Caleb leaned over the table. "Holly?"

"Yes?"

"I asked you if you were okay?"

"I… I think so." She released a slow breath. "I'm unbelievably nervous." She held out her hand so he could see how it shook. She shrugged. "The alcohol helps. I guess."

Caleb snorted. "Not always." He pushed a glass of water closer to her. "Drink some of that."

Holly sipped the water, closed her eyes, and took a deep breath. "I'm sorry. You must be regretting this … date. I called you an attention whore—"

"You didn't say that." He laughed. "Obviously, you were thinking it though."

"Like I said, you must be regretting this."

Caleb winked. "No, I'm not. I enjoy being here with you."

Holly swallowed her surprise. "Can we start over? Pretend the last ten minutes didn't happen?"

Caleb chuckled. "Do you want to go outside and come back in?"

Holly laughed. "Would it help if I did? Because I would seriously consider it." She shifted in her seat. "You know what? I am going to go to the restroom, splash some water on my face, and try to get myself together. I'll be right back."

Before Caleb could answer, she pushed herself out of her seat and darted down the hall leading to the restrooms. Inside, she closed the door and breathed a sigh of relief when the lock clicked in place. She leaned against it and closed her eyes.

I am an idiot. I shouldn't be here.

People like her didn't date the hottest celebrity in the world. Right now, she wanted to get through the evening and get home with her dignity intact. Maybe if she tried hard enough, she could get through the meal without making a bigger fool of herself.

Chapter Seven

HOLLY

When Holly came out of the bathroom, she stopped dead in her tracks. An older woman and a young girl stood at the table beside Caleb. She watched as he got up, took a picture with them, and chatted for a minute or so before they went back to their own table. She squared her shoulders and returned to the table.

As she sat down, Lou appeared with their food. Everything looked and smelled amazing. She thanked Lou and picked up her fork. They ate in silence.

"You're awfully quiet," Caleb whispered after a few minutes.

Holly shrugged. She couldn't argue with him. He was right. She hadn't said more than ten words since she returned from the bathroom. She didn't want to say something stupid again. Unfortunately, her silence made everything awkward.

Caleb tried repeatedly and unsuccessfully to get her to talk. They finished their food, and the silence became more overwhelming. After a few seconds, Caleb sighed and excused himself to say hello to Lou's father, Joe.

Holly contemplated leaving, skipping out before Caleb came back, but the manners her mother instilled in her kept her from rushing out the door.

She clutched her phone in her hand, her finger hovering over the Uber app. If she asked for it now, it would be here by the time

Caleb returned. She could thank him, put this night behind her, and forget what a fool she'd been.

"Would you like to go for a walk?" Caleb asked from behind her.

Holly jumped, her phone falling to the table. Caleb grabbed it and handed it to her. "There's a great ice cream place down the street. We could go grab a scoop. If you'd like to, that is."

"I don't know. Aren't you done being nice to me and putting up with my intense awkwardness? I would think you'd be ready to get rid of me by now. This night has been a disaster."

Caleb laughed. "No, Holly, I'm not done being nice to you. I'm not just being nice to you. I *like* spending time with you."

Holly scoffed and shook her head. "Why do you like spending time with me? I insulted you, I'm awkward, and I'm not your type."

"I think you might be just my type. For the first time in forever, I feel like I can be myself. You make me feel normal."

"And you don't think this date has been a disaster?"

Caleb chuckled. "Trust me, this is far from the most disastrous date I've had." He held his hand out to her. "Come on, let's get some ice cream."

Caleb kept a hold of her hand even after he helped her out of the seat. They waved goodbye to Lou on their way out the door.

They walked three blocks down the street to May's Ice Cream Shoppe. The shop was cute, painted in bright colors. A long counter with pink and blue stools dominated the room. There were a few tables scattered around the room. Rows and rows of ice cream filled the cold case, every flavor imaginable on display.

"I love this place," Caleb said. "It's one of my favorites. I've been coming here since I was a kid."

"It's adorable. I love it."

"I love little shops like this. Like yours. They are the heart of America. They're the best part of the world." Caleb cleared his throat. "How many scoops?"

Holly held up her finger. "One, please. Vanilla."

Caleb smiled and winked. "One scoop of vanilla it is. Why don't you find us a table? In the back, maybe?" He glanced around the crowded room. "It might be more private back there."

"Sure."

Holly weaved through the tables to the back of the shop and sat at a table near the back door. She folded her hands in front of her and contemplated how she could graciously excuse herself.

She'd taken up enough of Caleb's time. She grabbed her phone and ordered an Uber. According to the app, she had ten minutes to eat her ice cream and say goodbye.

"There you go," Caleb said as he slid a dish of vanilla ice cream onto the table in front of her.

"Thanks." Holly shifted uneasily in her chair and glanced at the door before she picked up her spoon and dug into the sweet cream. She noticed two girls—pre-teens from the looks of them—staring at Caleb and whispering, their phones in their hands. She was going to mention it to Caleb, but he cleared his throat, drawing her attention away from the two girls.

"Holly, what's wrong?"

She shook her head. "Nothing."

Caleb raised an eyebrow. "Something has to be wrong. You look like you want to bolt. In fact, you've looked like you want to take off for most of the last hour." He set his spoon beside his bowl and leaned over the table. "Do you not want to be here?"

Holly sighed. "I don't know. I thought I wanted to be here. I'm just..." She squeezed her eyes shut and concentrated on saying the right thing. "Look, I was afraid to go out with you. I told you, I feel like I'm in over my head. In fact, the water is rising, and I'm drowning. This is so crazy, so weird, so surreal. It's not real life. People like me don't date people like you. People like me don't get to hang out with celebrities. I'm the girl hanging out on the sidelines, fangirling over the cute guy in the movie or on the cover of a magazine. I'm not the girl who gets the guy."

Caleb opened his mouth, but before he could say anything, Holly heard a commotion at the front door of the ice cream shop.

"What the hell?" she mumbled. She turned in her chair, but Caleb grabbed her hand before she saw anything.

"Don't turn around. We need to go."

He shot to his feet and dragged her out of her chair. They stumbled toward the back door as the paparazzi shouted questions after them.

"Caleb, who's the girl?"

"Where's Anne Marie?"

"Why are you cheating on your girlfriend?"

"Caleb, can we get a quick picture?"

They burst out the back door and hurried down the alley toward the street. Holly didn't know where they were going. A few minutes later, they stopped beneath a streetlight several blocks from the ice cream shop.

Caleb pulled his phone out and typed a quick message. "I texted Alex. He'll come get us, and we'll get you home."

Holly pulled her hand out of Caleb's grip and shook her head. "You know what? I already called an Uber. I was going to take off as soon as it arrived." Out of the corner of her eye, she saw several photographers—paparazzi—headed their way.

"I can take you home," Caleb said.

The paparazzi yelled Caleb's name. Persistent and annoying. She wasn't cut out for this. Dating a celebrity came with a set of rules she didn't know. Rules no one prepared her to follow.

Holly backed away and fumbled her phone from her purse. One look told her the Uber she ordered was around the corner. "Really, Caleb, it's okay. You take care of yourself, get yourself home. I'll talk to you later." She spun around and took off, ignoring Caleb yelling after her.

According to a press release, actor Caleb Peters enjoyed an evening out with a close friend. Mr. Peters and his friend spent the evening eating dinner at a family friend's restaurant, followed by ice cream at May's Ice Cream Shoppe. It was a nice evening shared with friends. Rumors of a supposed relationship between the two are inaccurate. Out of respect for his friend's desire for privacy, her name will not be released to the press.

At least it wasn't as bad as she thought it would be. She expected to wake up to her face plastered all over the internet, and not for good reasons. Instead, the only photos were of the back of her head. Nobody knew who she was. Even the statement Caleb released about their date left her name out, stating it had been a "nice evening shared between friends." That must be Hollywood for "terrible first date."

Holly shoved the tablet across the table, slumped in her seat, and shut her eyes. She didn't want to look at it anymore. Her stress levels were still off the charts. She'd barely slept. Instead, she laid awake, staring at the ceiling and replaying every stupid thing she'd said and done on their date. She was glad it was over.

"It's not that bad."

Holly jumped, her chair tipping precariously to one side. She grabbed the edge of the desk and glared at Zoe. "You scared the crap out of me."

"Sorry. But like I said, it's not that bad. He said you were friends."

"I don't even think we're that. I'm more like a … coworker, I guess. I think our date last night—if you can even call it that—proved that. Caleb Peters is out of my league. But it's okay. I'm not looking to date anybody, especially a celebrity. That could only end in disaster."

Zoe eased into the seat across from her. "You know there's more to Caleb than being a celebrity, right?"

Holly narrowed her eyes and shrugged. "If you say so."

"You should give him a chance."

"A chance? To what, date me?" Holly snorted. "I doubt he wants to date me. Last night was nothing more than a thank you dinner, Zoe." She pointed at the tablet on the desk. "I think his statement proves it. He's not interested in anything more." She pushed herself upright. "I guarantee you the two of us dating will not come up again. From here on out, it will be strictly business between us."

Chapter Eight

CALEB

His date with Holly *was* a disaster. He tried to convince her it wasn't, but deep down, he couldn't even convince himself. She was on edge all night, obviously uncomfortable, and he didn't know how to calm her down or help her relax. Once she thought she offended him, it was all downhill. He couldn't seem to bring it back around.

His suggestion to get ice cream helped. Holly talked to him, explained why she was so nervous, and for the first time all night, they made progress. Of course, thanks to his dumb luck, the paparazzi arrived, and an unpleasant situation got worse. Holly couldn't get away fast enough. He stood there and watched her run away down the street.

For a split second, he contemplated chasing her, but the paparazzi would have followed him, and it would have turned into a mess he couldn't fix. So he stayed put.

The paparazzi surrounded him, shouting questions from every direction. He dropped his head and stared at the ground. Alex swooped in a few minutes later, ushered him into the car, and they drove away.

Caleb slumped in the passenger seat with his hand over his eyes.

"That bad, huh?" Alex asked.

"It wasn't great."

"What happened?"

"Nothing specific, aside from the usual paparazzi attack. It was just... I don't know if I remember how to date like a normal person. I worried about the paparazzi, worried about being recognized, worried about everything that comes with being Caleb Peters. I didn't worry about Holly. Well, I did, but not like I should have. I don't know. It was a train wreck."

"Maybe you're wrong. Maybe it's not that bad—"

"She ran away, Alex. Wouldn't let me give her a ride home, wouldn't even say much for most of the night. It was a disaster."

Alex sighed and shook his head. "Call her tomorrow and see if you can salvage things. It might not be that bad."

Caleb shrugged. "I'll think about it."

Alex faced forward, knowing full well there was no use arguing with his brother. Caleb stared out the window, wondering if he could fix this.

Who is Caleb Peter's Mystery Woman?

The headline screamed at him from The Gossip Monger's website. He shouldn't have looked at it; he should have known they would twist his simple date into something it wasn't. But the compulsion to see what the press was saying about him wouldn't go away. It was an itch he always had to scratch.

He tossed his phone on the couch and scrubbed a hand over his face. Holly wasn't a mystery woman. She was a sweet, wonderful woman he wanted to get to know better. Unfortunately, his lifestyle didn't allow him to date a normal woman. He couldn't have anything easy or good in his life, not when he was one of the most popular actors in the world. He'd tried, but it was not possible.

Caleb's eyes drifted to the bar in the corner. God, he could use a drink. He shoved to his feet, crossed the room, and opened the mini fridge. Water, Coke, and a few Red Bulls. He exhaled and grabbed a Red Bull. Alex must have stocked it.

His cell phone chimed from the middle of the bed. He snatched it up.

[Paul: I released a statement about your date with Holly.]

Caleb sighed and typed out an answer.

[Caleb: Already? That was quick.]

[Paul: I wanted to get ahead of it. Next time, a little heads up would be nice.]

[Caleb: Sorry. I didn't expect it to turn into this.]

[Paul: It always turns into this. You should know that by now. By the way, I need to see the location of the party. I need to make sure it's going to work.]

Caleb sent a thumbs up emoji and promised to get back to his agent with a time to visit Holly's shop. He pulled up The Gossip Monger website and saw the statement from Paul. It wasn't perfect, and it wasn't what he would have said, but it would do. At least it said nothing derogatory about Holly or even identified her.

He took a deep breath and sent a text to Holly.

[Caleb: Can we talk?]

Caleb pulled his hat down and adjusted his sunglasses. He watched the street, waiting for a lull in pedestrian traffic before he went inside. It was early, a few minutes after nine, so there weren't many people out. As soon as the street emptied, he shoved open the door.

"Wait here," he told Tiny before he climbed out of the SUV.

Inside, he headed straight for the bakery counter. The girl who worked with Holly popped up from behind the display case, a smile on her face.

"Hi! You're Caleb Peters, right?" She stood on her tiptoes and reached over the counter. "I'm Zoe."

Caleb glanced over his shoulder before shaking her hand. He put a finger to his mouth. "Shh. I'm trying to fly under the radar here."

"Oh my God, I'm so sorry." She dropped her voice to a conspiratorial whisper. "Are you here to see Holly?"

"I am," he whispered back. "Is she available?"

Zoe nodded. "Follow me."

She gestured for him to follow her through a swinging door and ushered him into a large industrial kitchen. Six ovens lined the back wall. Another wall held two large glass-front refrigerators filled with baked goods. The most incredible smells filled the room. Holly stood with her back to him in front of a sink full of bubbles.

"Holly?"

She swung around, bubbles dripping on the floor by her feet, a squeak leaving her when she saw Caleb. She'd pulled her hair back in a low ponytail, wisps of hair framing her face. Her hazel eyes widened in surprise. "Caleb? What are you doing here?"

He chuckled. "Well, hello to you, too."

Holly twittered nervously and wiped her hands on the apron around her waist. "Sorry. Hello, Caleb. What are you doing here?"

"I came by to apologize for last night. I am so sorry about... well, about everything. The awkward dinner conversation, the paparazzi, me."

Holly took a step closer to him, seemed to think twice about it, stopped, and rested her hand on the counter. "You shouldn't apologize. I'm the one who stuck my foot in my mouth and acted like an idiot. I think I went in with some crazy expectations, and when it wasn't like I thought it would be, I didn't know how to act."

"Crazy expectations?"

"You're a celebrity, Caleb..."

Caleb waved his hand and shook his head. "I know I'm a celebrity. You know I'm a celebrity. For five minutes, I'd like to forget all of that."

"That's hard to do when people are snapping pictures of you during dinner, following us into the ice cream shop, and chasing us down the alley."

"I know," Caleb muttered. "It was rough. Dealing with the paparazzi is a nightmare." He pinched the bridge of his nose and exhaled. "I'm sorry you had to put up with that."

"It's not your fault. You don't control them, right?"

He chuckled. "I wish I did. It would make my life easier."

Holly smiled, but it looked disingenuous. "Excuse me, Caleb. I don't mean to be rude, but aside from offering me an apology, did you want something?"

Caleb sighed heavily. "Let me make it up to you."

"Make it up to me how?" Holly asked warily.

"I'd like to take you out again—"

Holly cut him off. "I'm not interested in dating you, Caleb. I'm not interested in dating *anyone*, to be honest. I don't need you to fix anything. I don't need a make-up date."

"Okay…"

"I think we should concentrate on making your party the best experience we can. That's what's important right now. Don't you agree?"

Caleb nodded. "Yeah. Sure." He cleared his throat. "You know what might help?"

Holly shook her head, her eyebrows raised. "What do you think would help?"

"I think it would help if you got to know me better. Don't you? If we got to be friends, planning my party with Tiara would be easier."

Her eyes narrowed, and she put her hands on her hips. "I guess so."

"So, will you go out with me on Sunday afternoon? I know where we can go, where no one treats me like a celebrity."

"That's what you said about that Italian restaurant we went to last night. And you know how that ended."

He did, and it irked him to no end. He'd promised her a good, drama-free evening, and he hadn't given it to her. This was his last desperate attempt to prove to her they could have a good time and he wasn't some irritating, snobby celebrity. There was only one place he could take her where she could see he was just a normal guy.

"Trust me. Where I plan to take you, I impress no one with my celebrity status. No one. Please come with me. We'll have fun, and you can see a side of me nobody ever gets to see. Well, nobody unimportant anyway."

"Sunday afternoon?" she asked.

"Yep." He stepped closer. "Is that a yes?"

"Um, yeah, I guess. I'll have to ask Zoe to cover my shift—"

"I can do it," Zoe shouted from the other side of the swinging door.

Holly rolled her eyes, and Caleb laughed. "Great. I'll have Tiny pick you up on Sunday around eleven."

"Tiny?"

"He's one of my bodyguards. I'd do it myself, but…" He shrugged and didn't finish his sentence. "I'm sorry." Instead of proving there was more to him than being a celebrity, he was reiterating it by sending his bodyguard to pick Holly up for a date.

Holly cleared her throat and stared at the ceiling. "You know what? Maybe we should forget it. You can have your party here, and I'll do whatever I need to do to help you with that. Tiara can fill me in on whatever I need to know. When the party is over, we'll go our separate ways."

Caleb crossed the small kitchen in two strides and put a hand on Holly's arm. "Please, Holly. Come with me on Sunday afternoon. If I blow it, I swear I won't ask you out again."

She hesitated long enough that Caleb thought she was going to say no. He held his breath while he waited for her answer.

"Alright, I'll go."

Caleb exhaled and grinned. "You won't regret it. I promise." He squeezed Holly's arm and gave her a warm smile. "I'll see you on Sunday." He turned to leave, but Holly stopped him with a question.

"By the way, where are we going?"

He turned around slowly and grinned at her. He cleared his throat and adjusted his hat. "Dinner at my parents."

"Wait a minute. You're asking me to a family dinner? I don't know, Caleb. That sounds weird."

"I know it's weird. But it will be quiet and free from paparazzi. I figured a family gathering with no press or fans or all that other crap might be a good way to start. Or start again, I guess. If you don't want to, I understand."

He saw the war of indecision in Holly's eyes, so it surprised him when she nodded.

"Okay, I'll go. If you're honest with me about something."

Crap. I don't like the sound of that.

"Alright, what is it?"

"Is this another date? I know you said it isn't, but I get the distinct impression that, to you, it is."

Caleb scratched the back of his neck and chuckled under his breath. "Um … busted."

"Caleb—"

"I know you're not interested in dating. You made that perfectly clear. How about I take my new friend Holly to meet my family? Is that okay?"

"Wow, you're good. Now we're friends?"

"We can be. If it's okay with you."

"You drive a hard bargain, but I guess I can handle being friends. For now. I'll go to your parents with you on Sunday, as a friend."

There was silence for a second before Caleb whooped so loud Holly winced. "Great! That's… that's great." He cleared his throat. "Okay, so Tiny will pick you up on Sunday at eleven."

"I can't wait," she said. He noted she didn't sound excited.

Caleb kissed Holly on the cheek, winked, spun around, and left without another word. He had some phone calls to make before Sunday.

Chapter Nine

HOLLY

The shop phone rang just after closing on Saturday night. Holly contemplated not answering it, but the need to put her customers first overrode her need to ignore the call.

Caleb was on the other end. She wasn't expecting to hear from him, not when she was supposed to see him the next day.

"Hello," she stammered, standing there with the phone clutched tightly in one hand and her other gripping the edge of the counter.

"I wanted to apologize again for the other night," he said. "And make sure you're still coming tomorrow."

"I'll be there." Her hands shook at the thought of meeting Caleb's parents. "Should I dress up or anything—"

"Nah, it's just a family dinner. Me, my parents, my brothers, and my brother's wife. Dress comfortably. My dad might try to drag you into a doubles badminton tournament."

Holly laughed nervously. It wasn't just his parents; it was the whole damn family. Shit. "Okay. I guess I'll see you tomorrow." She said goodbye and carefully dropped the phone back into the cradle. Her head swam.

"What the hell am I going to wear?" she muttered under her breath.

Dark jeans and a lightweight green sweater ended up being the most comfortable thing she could find. She pulled her honey-blonde hair into a low ponytail and tied it with a matching green ribbon.

True to her word, Zoe showed up to cover the shop for the five hours it was open on Sunday. For once, she was early, a huge grin on her face as she settled at the front counter.

"Nervous?" she asked.

"Of course, I'm nervous. I'm meeting Caleb Peters' parents."

That thought had run through her head all morning—while she got ready, while she drank three cups of coffee, while she paced at the front of the shop. She stopped every few seconds to peer out the window, bouncing on her toes, her fingers tapping against the side of her leg.

I'm meeting Caleb Peters' parents.

Multiple times over the last few hours, she considered calling Caleb and canceling. She could pretend to be sick or maybe say Zoe couldn't cover her shift. Anything to get out of going with Caleb. She had a chance to do it last night, and she chickened out. She wasn't sure she could endure an afternoon and evening with his family. Meeting parents was one thing, but meeting the parents of a famous actor was an entirely unique thing. What if they didn't like her? What if they didn't think she was good enough to be with Caleb?

That's okay because I'm not with Caleb. We're friends.

When Holly expressed these thoughts to Zoe, her friend rolled her eyes. "It's not like you're marrying him. Try to relax."

"Easy for you to say," Holly muttered.

Zoe laughed. "I know. But seriously, calm down. Yes, you're meeting Caleb Peters' parents. Try to look at it for what it is. You're meeting the parents of a guy who is interested in you."

"He's not interested in me," Holly said with a scoff. "We're friends."

Zoe snorted. "Um, are you blind? That boy has it bad."

Holly rolled her eyes. "We're friends," she reiterated. "He's using the shop for a party. That's it. Nothing more. He isn't interested in me."

"Okay, whatever you say. Let's agree to disagree. Still, take a deep breath and relax. I'm sure Caleb's parents treat him like a normal person. Because that's what he is. Just a normal guy with parents and brothers. Stop worrying about the celebrity side of it and try to enjoy yourself."

At eleven a.m. on the dot, a black SUV pulled to a stop in front of the shop. Caleb's driver stepped out, smiled at Holly through the window, and waved.

Holly looked at Zoe over her shoulder and forced a smile onto her face. "Wish me luck." She opened the door and stepped out.

"Good luck!" Zoe called after her.

Caleb's driver chuckled and shook his head. He held out his hand. "Ms. Wright? I'm Tiny."

Holly shook his hand. "Nice to meet you, Tiny. In case I forget, thanks for the ride. And please, call me Holly."

"Holly it is. And you're welcome. Front or back?"

"Oh goodness, please don't make me sit in the back. I'll feel ridiculous."

Tiny laughed and opened the front passenger door. She climbed in and buckled up.

"Are you nervous?" he asked after he pulled into traffic. "I only ask because—"

"Because my leg won't quit shaking? Or because my fingers won't stop tapping? My friend screaming 'good luck' out the door? Which is it?"

"All the above." Tiny gave her a gentle smile. "Trust me, you'll be fine."

"Tell that to my stomach that's tied in knots." She folded her hands in her lap and squeezed them together so hard they hurt.

"It helps if you remember Caleb is just an ordinary guy."

Holly sighed. "Everybody keeps saying that."

"Because it's true. Trust me, he's a giant goofball. At least according to his brother, Alex."

Holly tipped her head to one side. "You know his brother?"

"Yeah, of course. Big guy, tattoos, muscles? Follows Caleb everywhere? He picked Caleb up the day he got trapped in your store, and he was with him last week when he stopped in. That's Alex."

Holly laughed. "I thought that was his bodyguard."

"Oh, he is Caleb's bodyguard. Brother and bodyguard."

"I had no idea." She exhaled. "Between you and me, what do you really think of Caleb?"

"Caleb is a good guy. He's had his troubles, made mistakes, but when it comes down to brass tacks, he's funny, down-to-earth, and a great actor. His family grounds him. They're extremely important to him. He wouldn't want you to meet them if he didn't like you."

"Great. That doesn't help my nerves."

Tiny laughed. "Sorry. Try to relax and have fun. It's hard not to around Caleb's family."

They made small talk as they drove out of town. An hour later, Tiny turned down a dirt drive and came to a stop in front of a large rambling farmhouse.

Tiny parked, jumped out, and ran around the front of the car to open the door before she could. He took Holly's hand and helped her from the SUV.

"Wow," she whispered. "This place is gorgeous."

"It's been in the family for forty years. Jack and Wendy inherited it from Jack's parents. Jack runs the ranch, and Wendy is a schoolteacher. See what I meant when I say they ground Caleb? Nothing fancy here."

"Holly!" Caleb appeared on the porch, hurried down the steps, and took her hand. "I'm so glad you're here. Thanks, Tiny."

"Any time," Tiny answered. "Remember, Holly, have fun. I'm gonna grab a drink."

"Dad has soda out back in the cooler. And he's looking for help with the badminton net."

"On it!" Tiny shouted over his shoulder.

"Tiny's staying?" Holly asked.

Caleb nodded. "He and Alex are friends. And my mom adores him." He squeezed her hand. "Hi."

"Hi." She hated the way her voice got high and squeaky. She cleared her throat. "You know, I really do appreciate the invitation, but won't this be weird? I mean, you and I just met. This is your family. I'm sure they would rather spend time with you without some strange woman hanging around."

"You'll be a refreshing change from the last few women I've dated. Come on, let's go meet my family." He dragged her up the stairs and into the house.

Caleb's family turned out to be nothing short of amazing. His mother, Wendy, was a raven-haired beauty and small in stature, especially compared to her sons. All the boys towered over their mother, each of them standing at over six feet. But Wendy was a force to be reckoned with and good at keeping her boys in line.

It was obvious that Caleb and his brothers got their height from their father, Jack. He was an intimidating presence, unbelievably tall with a deep, gruff voice. But the gruffness ended there. He shook Holly's hand and offered her a drink with a grin and a wink.

"It's nice to meet you, Holly," he said. "Caleb said you own a bookstore?"

She nodded. "I do. A bookstore and a bakery."

"So no acting?"

Holly laughed. "No, no acting. In fact, I'm terrible at it. I failed drama in high school."

Jack burst out laughing. "You don't know how glad I am to hear that."

"Dad," Caleb interrupted. "Enough! Your daughter-in-law is going to hear you."

"Shit, you're right." Jack laughed and winked at Holly. "Don't tell Miranda I said that."

Before she could say "Miranda, who?" Caleb grabbed her hand and tugged her toward the kitchen door.

"Come on. You can meet my brothers."

Holly followed Caleb to the backyard. He introduced her to Rylan, who was setting up the badminton net with Tiny.

"Holly, this is Rylan. He's the middle brother and the butt of all the jokes."

"Ha, ha, you're funny." Rylan shook Holly's hand. "It's nice to meet you. I have to ask: how much is he paying you to be here?"

Holly's mouth dropped open. "Um..."

Caleb punched Rylan in the arm. "Ignore him. He's just jealous I have an attractive date and he's stuck with Tiny."

Holly burst out laughing along with Tiny and Rylan. She waved at them over her shoulder as Caleb led her across the yard.

"One left," Caleb said. "Don't let Alex intimidate you. He's sweeter than he looks."

The big, tattooed guy Holly had seen with Caleb last week sat at a picnic table with a gorgeous woman who looked vaguely familiar.

"Holly, you know Alex. He's not just my bodyguard; he's my big brother."

Alex rose to his feet and shook Holly's hand. "It's nice to meet you officially. I don't think Caleb introduced us before. His parents obviously didn't raise him well."

The woman sitting with Alex stood up and punched him in the arm. "Alex, be nice. Your parents are saints. Don't disparage their name." She turned to Holly. "Hi, Holly. I'm Miranda, Alex's wife."

"Holy shit, you're Miranda Putnam," Holly blurted then immediately slapped her hand over her mouth.

Christ, I need a muzzle.

Miranda laughed. "Yes, I am."

"Wow, there are actors all over this place," Holly muttered. "Actors and bodyguards. I'm going to make a fool of myself for sure."

Miranda giggled, then Alex laughed, followed by Caleb. Before she knew it, they'd filled the backyard with the sound of joyous, raucous laughter.

Some of the tension went out of her shoulders. She could do this; everyone was nice, down-to-earth, and easy to talk to, even the insanely gorgeous Miranda. The whole family welcomed her with open arms. Wendy made a point of including her in their conversations, and Jack insisted she join the family badminton tournament being held in the backyard.

Her favorite thing about the family meal with the Peters was the way they treated Caleb and Miranda. To Holly's surprise, Miranda voluntarily cleared the table, and Caleb helped Alex load the dishwasher. She supposed in Jack and Wendy's home, Caleb and Miranda were just a son and a daughter-in-law, not movie stars earning multi-million-dollar paychecks. After a while, Holly forgot she was hanging out with movie stars.

Caleb and his brothers had her laughing constantly, and their banter kept a permanent smile on her face. His parents were wonderful and obviously in love. Even Tiny had a playful streak. The day flew by, and before she knew it, the sun had set, and it was time to go home.

Jack squeezed her hand as he shook it and gave her a warm smile. "Don't be a stranger, Holly." His voice dropped to a whisper. "We really like you."

Holly grinned. "Thank you, Mr. Peters. I can't tell you how great that makes me feel. I hope to see you again." Of course, only Caleb could decide to bring her around again.

Wendy surprised her by giving her a hug goodbye, reiterating Jack's request. Holly laughed and promised to do her best.

Once Holly said her goodbyes, Caleb sent her to find Tiny. He promised to catch up with her after he talked to his parents.

Holly followed Tiny outside and waved goodbye to Miranda and Alex sitting on the porch. Miranda bounded to her feet and stepped in front of Holly.

"Can we get lunch sometime?"

"Um, yeah, I guess so." Holly looked around then leaned close to Miranda. "You know, you don't have to be nice to me because of Caleb," she whispered.

Miranda giggled and shook her head. "I'm not being nice to you because of Caleb. I would love to get to know you more. You're far more interesting than any other woman Caleb has ever brought around. Definitely better than Anne—"

"Miranda!" Alex interjected.

"Sorry," she mouthed. She squeezed Holly's upper arm. "I'll come by your shop one day. You can show me around, and we'll grab lunch. Okay?"

"I'd like that," Holly responded. She would, too. Miranda was sweet and funny, and Holly would love to get to know her better.

Tiny opened the door to the SUV with a flourish. "Ms. Wright, let's get you home," he called.

"Tiny, wait!" Caleb darted out the front door and sprinted down the porch steps. "I think I'll take Holly home."

"Are you sure?" Alex followed his brother off the porch. He stopped in front of Caleb, his arms crossed over his chest, biceps bulging, and one eyebrow raised. "Tiny can do it."

Caleb nodded. "I'm sure. I want to take her home. I'll take the Galaxie. No one will know it's me."

Alex nodded, but his pinched face and narrowed eyes gave away how he really felt. He whispered something to Tiny, who nodded, gave Holly a one-armed hug, then went back into the farmhouse without another word.

"Be careful, Caleb," Alex said, wagging his finger in his brother's face. "I mean it. Don't do anything stupid."

Caleb rolled his eyes, but he nodded at his brother. "I won't. I promise."

"Take her home and then come straight back. Tiny is going to stay here. He'll take you back to your hotel in the morning."

"Yes, sir," Caleb muttered. "Can I go now?"

Alex nodded and squeezed Holly's upper arm. "It was great to meet you, Holly. I hope this isn't the last time we see you." He gave his brother a pointed look before heading back inside.

Caleb gestured for Holly to follow him. "Come on, let's go."

Chapter Ten

CALEB

Holly cleared her throat. "Did I hear you say you have a Galaxie?"

Caleb nodded. "I did. A 1965 Ford Galaxie."

Holly's eyes widened. "No way. God, I love the '65 Galaxie. My grandpa had a black one. I loved that car. Unfortunately, he sold it when I was in high school. I was so upset I couldn't talk to him for weeks. I'd planned to buy it from him when I was old enough to drive."

He loved listening to her talk. The sudden sharing of information took him by surprise. He was glad he'd asked her to family dinner; they'd had a lot of fun.

"Earth to Caleb?" Holly poked him in the bicep. "Is yours a convertible?"

"Sorry. I zoned out for a second. She *is* a convertible. And she is gorgeous, a real beauty." A smile spread across his face as he talked about his car. She was the one thing he owned in this world that was all his, and he was proud of her. He bought her when he was eighteen with his first big paycheck. Then, when all of his problems began, he moved her to his parents' place to keep her safe. Working on her, keeping her in mint condition, was cathartic. It gave him an escape.

"Do you want to see her?" he asked.

Holly bounced on her toes. "I would love to!"

"Come on. She's in the barn." He loved any opportunity to show off the Galaxie, especially when it was to someone who might appreciate her as much as he did.

Caleb took Holly's hand and led her around the back of the huge red barn next to the house. It was the perfect place to keep the Galaxie. She was out of the elements, out of Dad's way, and out of sight of any paparazzi who might wander near the property. So far, he'd kept the car out of the public eye, which meant he could drive it whenever he wanted.

He pushed open the door and took Holly into the dark, dusty barn. Sitting under the window was his tarp-covered car. He dropped Holly's hand, threw the switch by the door to turn on the light, hurried to the car, and yanked off the tarp with a flourish.

Holly stopped dead in her tracks. "Wow!"

Caleb grinned. At that moment, he knew she loved his car. He saw it written all over her face. Her eyes lit up, and a smile brightened her face, somehow making her even prettier. Her eyes roved over every inch of the Galaxie's perfect exterior. He'd spent hours meticulously looking for dings or chips in the paint and cleaning her with a soft cloth. The look on Holly's face made it all worthwhile.

As he watched, she reached out to touch the car, stopping short of placing her hand on the hood. She glanced over at Caleb, waiting for his permission.

Damn it, that's the hottest thing I've ever seen a woman do.

Caleb nodded and watched closely as she placed her hand on the car's hood. He didn't realize he wasn't breathing until she rubbed her hand over the smooth surface. He released a slow, controlled breath.

"She's stunning," Holly whispered.

The smile on his face widened.

"She is, isn't she?" Caleb's brain shifted into car mode, a subject he never tired of discussing. He launched into a detailed description of the Galaxie's specs, forgetting who he was talking to. After a few minutes, he realized he was probably boring Holly to tears. Except, when he looked up at her, she was smiling and nodding. It was obvious she was listening intently to everything he said.

"I didn't know you were into cars," Holly said.

"There are a lot of things you don't know about me. I have my reputation as a mystery man for a reason. I keep things close to the chest. I'm surprised you didn't guess it when you guessed my book type."

Holly blinked several times before looking down. She caressed the car's vinyl top. "Are you taking me home in this?"

"I am," Caleb said.

The smile on Holly's face made his heart skip a beat and his stomach twist. He had to stop himself from grabbing her and kissing her.

Holly's knowledge of cars surprised Caleb. She knew at least as much as he did, if not more. They discussed her love of old cars, how it had come about, and how she knew so much. It was all thanks to her grandfather and her father, both of whom loved cars and passed that love onto Holly.

One subject bled into another, and Caleb asked her more questions to get her to talk. She told him about her multiple attempts at school—regular and culinary—and her decision to open the baking and book shop. She even hinted at the problems the shop was having and how she hoped Caleb's party would bail her out. After a moment of awkward silence, she turned the subject to him, insisting he tell her why he'd chosen to act as a profession.

Caleb laughed and shook his head. "You don't want to hear about that. It's old news. You can probably Google it."

"I *have* Googled it," Holly replied. "But I want to hear it from you."

He rolled his eyes, but he found he wanted to tell her. "Both of my brothers are bodyguards."

"Both of them? I thought it was just Alex."

"Nope," Caleb said. "Alex *and* Rylan are both bodyguards. I hung out with them a few times while they worked on small stuff like on-set protection. I got bit by the acting bug. One of Alex's clients pulled some strings and got me a small part in one of his movies. I think I was eighteen or nineteen. Next thing I knew, I had an agent and piles of scripts coming to the house. I had my pick of anything I wanted to do. The rest is history."

"I think you're being modest." Holly smiled, reached across the seat, and squeezed his hand. "You wouldn't have the career you do without a lot of hard work. It couldn't have been easy."

She had no idea. The stress had taken its toll, and it had nearly destroyed him. But it wasn't something he was ready to discuss with Holly. Not when they'd only know each other for a short time. He still wasn't sure she liked him. She'd had fun with his family, but how she felt about him was still a mystery.

Caleb focused on the road, occasionally sneaking glances at Holly out of the corner of his eye. According to his family, she wasn't his type. Rylan—the family spokesperson—made a point of pulling him aside after dinner to ask him about Holly. Her ability to stand her ground around the Peters family surprised them. They weren't used to him being with someone who was smart, driven, and sarcastic.

"We like her," Rylan told him. "It's just that she's not the type of girl you usually date."

His brothers and the rest of the world thought his type was the into-herself, stuck-up diva princess, not a reserved, bookish baker who owned her own business. Of course, he had no one to blame for that except himself; he'd spent years cultivating an image, and that image included dating some of Hollywood's most sought after women. But he'd never seen himself establishing any kind of lasting relationship with those women.

Holly was different. He could see himself with her.

But maybe Holly didn't like him, the *real* him. She probably wanted the gorgeous guy who graced multiple magazine covers, the guy everyone considered the bad-boy actor. Most women wanted the aloof, sexy, unattainable, Greek God persona he'd created and hid behind, not the damaged, flawed, nerdy, car-guy Caleb Peters. That Caleb wasn't the dream.

They were almost back to L.A. when it dawned on Caleb that he didn't know where he was going. He'd only been to Holly's shop. He didn't know where she lived.

"Where am I going? Where do you live?"

Holly sighed and shook her head. "I live above the shop."

"Really? There's an apartment upstairs? I never would have guessed."

"It's nothing special, just a tiny apartment. And I mean *tiny*. It's a studio apartment with a small kitchen and a great room with an attached bathroom. I put a sofa bed, a small table, and a chair up there. I had another apartment, but I was at the shop so much it seemed silly to go home every night. It was easier to move into the apartment upstairs. And cheaper. I've saved a ton of money since I let the lease on my apartment lapse."

They drove in silence until Caleb pulled into the alley behind her shop and shut off the car. He turned to Holly.

"Would you like to come in for a drink?" she asked, surprising him. He figured once he got her home, she would wrap up the date quickly. Inviting him in was a good sign.

Caleb chuckled nervously. "Um … coffee, maybe? Nothing too strong though. No alcohol."

He expected her to ask why he wasn't interested in a nightcap, but she didn't seem to care.

"I have some of the best coffee in the state. I also have some of the most amazing desserts you'll ever taste."

"I love dessert. What do you have?"

"Anything you want," she replied. "Cakes, cookies, pies, cupcakes. You name it, I probably have it. I mean, I *am* a baker."

Caleb winked. "That's right. You are."

"It could… well, I guess it could be a trial run for your party. You can taste test my baked goods, maybe decide what you'd like me to make." Holly shrugged. "Just a thought."

"Sounds like a great idea. I'd love to come in."

Caleb climbed from the car and followed Holly through the back entrance and inside. In the kitchen, he sat at a small table in the corner while Holly made coffee and pulled desserts from the fridge. He enjoyed watching her, talking to her, and being with her. He loved the sense of normalcy that came over him whenever she was around. He didn't have to pretend to be someone he wasn't.

"Tell me more about your shop," he said.

Holly finished putting together a small tray of treats for him to sample, then she set everything on the table and slid into the seat across from him.

"Long story short: I love to bake, and I love to read, so I put the two things together. It's an unusual business model, but I think it's unique. I've been trying to make it work for the last eighteen months."

"Is it working?" Caleb asked.

Holly sighed and shook her head. "I'm not making any money, if that's what you're asking. I'm struggling."

"Is my party going to help?"

She nodded. "I hope so. I need to get noticed. Hosting a party for the sexiest man alive should go a long way toward that." A shy grin danced across her lips. "I can't thank you enough. I'm not sure why you're doing it, but I really appreciate it."

"You're welcome. I'm happy to do it. And I hope it helps."

"Can I ask you a question?"

"Sure. I'm an open book."

"Why *are* you helping me? I'm sure there are a million places you could have your party, much better places than my little shop. I don't understand why you want to have it here."

"I like it here. It's fun and quirky and a unique place to have a party. And even though it's a private party, I think it will bring you a lot of attention."

"Well, thank you. You're very sweet. For a celebrity." Holly winked.

Caleb reached across the table, took her hands in his, and held them tight. He leaned close enough that he could smell her perfume. "Do you know why I asked you out?"

"To thank me for letting you use my shop for your party—"

Caleb waved away her answer. "I said that because I wasn't sure you'd go out with me. The real reason I asked you out is because I like how I feel when I'm with you. I don't have to pretend to be something I'm not. I get to be me. I haven't been able to do that for years. And I hope you like me for me, not because I'm some famous actor."

Holly swallowed and stared at their clasped hands. "I do like you," she whispered. "And not just because you're a celebrity. Though, I will admit, I had a hard time getting past your fame. I have certain preconceived notions about celebrities. Thanks to you and Miranda, those ideas are being called into question. Now that I've gotten to know you, I have to say you're not what I expected."

"I hope that's a good thing."

Holly squeezed his hands. "It is. I had a great time today. Your family is wonderful."

"They thought you were wonderful, too." Caleb grinned. "I'd like to go out again if you want to." He eased around the table, slipped into the chair beside her, and rested his arm on the back of her chair. His heart pounded, and he was sweating as he took her hand again.

"Let's have lunch tomorrow—just the two of us. You can come to my hotel."

Holly raised an eyebrow.

"I swear, just for lunch. It will give us a chance to talk and get to know each other better. Please? It's away from any crowds."

Holly smiled. "Okay, lunch tomorrow. I'll do my best to get over the fact that you are a celebrity, and you… well, I guess you have to act normal."

Caleb laughed. "Sounds like a deal." He tangled his fingers in her hair, cupped the back of her head, and pulled her close. He kissed her, nothing more than a slight brush of his lips against hers, but it was the most amazing kiss he'd had in ages. He didn't want it to end.

Unfortunately, his phone chose that moment to go off. They broke apart, and Caleb yanked it out of his pocket.

[Alex: Are you on your way home?]

Caleb chuckled and shook his head. "My brother. Always looking out for me." He took a hold of Holly's hand and rose to his feet, pulling her with him. He leaned over and kissed her again.

"Tomorrow, my hotel, one p.m. Ask the concierge for Rick Blaine's room."

Holly giggled. "Rick Blaine? Like from *Casablanca*?"

He nodded. "Exactly. I'll see you tomorrow." He kissed her one last time then quickly turned to leave. If he didn't go right then, he wouldn't leave at all. He'd stay with her all night if he could. As if to remind him he couldn't, his phone vibrated again. He laughed as he saw the line of angry emojis from Alex.

Not that he cared; he had another date with Holly. Tomorrow couldn't get here soon enough.

Chapter Eleven

HOLLY

The Beverly Hills Wilshire was one of the most opulent hotels in the city and the fanciest place Holly had ever been to. She checked her reflection in the huge front window before she went inside, feeling seriously underdressed in her jeans and blouse. Too late to do anything about it now.

At the concierge's desk, Holly asked for Rick Blaine's room. She expected him to laugh at her or maybe roll his eyes, but the concierge got a funny smile on his face—like she did when Caleb told her who to ask for—wrote two numbers on a slip of paper and handed it to her.

He pointed at the paper in her hand. "Punch that number into the keypad in the elevator, and it will take you to the correct floor. Turn left, and the room you are looking for will be right in front of you."

"Thanks," she whispered.

"You're very welcome, miss."

Holly put her head down and hurried across the lobby to the elevators. She tapped her fingers against her leg and hummed under her breath all the way to the eighth floor, her stomach twisting and turning with every floor she passed. Thank God no one was in the elevator with her.

The door to Caleb's room was ten quick steps from the elevator. She sucked in a deep breath and knocked on the door.

A full minute went by before Caleb yanked open the door, his brow furrowed and his teeth clenched. He shot a look over his shoulder and turned back to her.

His voice dropped to a low whisper. "I'm sorry, Holly, but we can't have lunch. Not today."

Over Caleb's shoulder, a beautiful woman emerged from a room along the long hallway. Her dark brown hair was in a high ponytail, and she wore a flowing white dress and cowboy boots. She walked up to Caleb, wrapped a hand around his bicep, and stared pointedly at Holly.

"Who are you?" she asked, eyeing Holly up and down.

Caleb cleared his throat and shot a glare at the young woman over his shoulder. "Be nice, Anne Marie. This is Holly. She owns a shop on Beverly Hills Drive. I'm using her place for an upcoming event." He didn't meet Holly's eyes as he spoke.

Holly forced a smile onto her face and held out her hand to the woman. She didn't know what was happening, but her deeply ingrained manners wouldn't allow her to be rude.

"It's nice to meet you. Anne Marie, right?"

Anne Marie stared at Holly's hand like she'd never seen one before. Saying nothing to Holly, she turned to Caleb. "Wow. Okay. Well, she has terrible timing. I made lunch reservations at the restaurant downstairs. Wrap up whatever it is you're doing and let's go." She glared at Holly, her hand resting possessively on Caleb's bicep, before she swung around and flitted away.

Holly stared after her, mouth ajar. She turned to Caleb. He shook his head and scrubbed a hand over the back of his neck.

"Who is that?" Holly whispered.

"That's uh… that's my … Anne Marie," Caleb mumbled. "The ex-girlfriend I told you about."

"If she's your ex-girlfriend, what is she doing in your hotel room?"

"Look, Holly, it's complicated. I can explain—just not right now."

Gutted, Holly grunted and took a step back. She gripped her bag so tightly her hands hurt.

"No need to explain," she spat. "I get it." She spun around and hurried back to the elevator.

Back at her store, Holly spent the day hiding in the kitchen. She baked and tried to forget what happened with Caleb. She was furious with both him and herself. She'd believed Caleb when he told her he and Anne Marie broke up. She got her hopes up and let herself believe Caleb when he said he was different. He didn't differ from any other asshole celebrity. Lesson learned.

By the time she closed the store and Zoe went home, the refrigerator was full of all kinds of goodies for the next day—cakes, cupcakes, a new muffin she'd been wanting to make, pies, and cookies.

Holly spent the night tossing and turning, unable to turn her brain off long enough to sleep. The stuff with Caleb had angered her more than she thought possible. How could she allow Caleb and his people to have a party in her store when he'd treated her so poorly?

Around three in the morning, she had a moment—a tear-filled, irrational moment—in which she considered canceling the party and refusing to help him. It would save her any more heartache.

Except Caleb's party would help her with business. She knew this with every fiber of her being. It would be colossally stupid to turn it down and walk away from it. While her heart ached, it wasn't broken. She would recover from the humiliation. From here on out, it would be a strictly professional relationship between her and Caleb. Nothing more.

Of course, when she woke, the first thing she saw on her phone was a text from Caleb. She deleted it without opening it. She wouldn't answer him; she would be professional. If he wanted to speak to her, it would be through either his agent or Tiara, the party planner.

Thinking about Tiara reminded Holly she had a meeting with her this morning. She dragged herself out of bed, washed her face, and pulled her hair into a ponytail. She didn't feel like dressing up, so she threw on a Bookish Bakery t-shirt, jeans, and her favorite beat-up Converse.

At ten a.m. on the dot, Tiara breezed through the door, a gigantic three-ring binder tucked under one arm and a large Michael Kors tote bag on the other arm. She went straight to the counter, sat down on a stool, and opened the binder.

"Are you ready to get started?" she asked.

Holly nodded. "We'll have to plan on the go. I gave my overworked assistant the day off, so I'm the only one running the show today."

"You only have one employee?"

Holly sighed. "Yes. Is that a problem?"

Tiara shook her head, but the look on her face and the rapid scribbling of her pen in the open binder said otherwise. "We'll have to bring in some help. For setting up, I mean. There's a lot of stuff that's going to have to be moved." She cleared her throat. "Are you going to be able to handle all the food? Caleb said you bake everything yourself?"

"I do," Holly replied. "I can handle it. I can bake anything." She pointed at the full display case. "I did most of that yesterday."

"Wow," Tiara mumbled. "That's impressive. Caleb wasn't kidding."

Holly scrubbed at the counter with a clean dishcloth. "Speaking of Caleb, will he be joining us?"

"No. He's busy. I doubt he'll be around much for the planning. If we have questions, I'll run it by him. Though, I think he and Paul are going to come by later this week. Paul wants to check things out." Tiara pointed at the coffeepot behind the counter. "Can I get a cup of that?"

Holly poured Tiara a cup of coffee and slid it across the counter. "What's next?"

"How attached to this layout are you?" Tiara waved a hand around the shop. "I'd like to make some changes, make it easier for everyone to walk around the night of the party. The changes might be beneficial to your flow of traffic on a day-to-day basis as well."

Holly nodded. "Okay. I guess. Is it going to be drastic?"

Tiara gave her a gentle smile. "No, I don't think so. Just minor changes that will make an enormous difference. Before I became a party planner to the stars, I worked in retail. I was head of visual merchandizing for a big company. If you hate it, move it back after the party. Does that sound good?"

"I think so, yeah."

Tiara leaned over the counter and caught Holly's eye. "You don't seem very excited about this. Are you okay?"

Holly contemplated her answer for a moment. "I don't know. I'm nervous about this and worried that I'm in over my head.

Caleb's a big deal. Maybe my little shop isn't the right place for a big Hollywood party."

Tiara put her hand on Holly's arm. "It's perfect, Holly. And I'm not just blowing smoke up your ass. This isn't the magazine launch party; it's a celebration for Caleb. He's in charge of the guest list and the size of the party. From what he's told me, he's not interested in some huge pre-party. He's interested in celebrating this accomplishment with his friends and his family. And this place is perfect for that. I know you think you're in over your head, but that's what I'm here for. The only thing you have to worry about is baking some amazing cakes and cookies and muffins and whatever else you make that smells so good." She took a deep breath. "Seriously, what is that glorious smell?"

Holly laughed, grabbed a cupcake from the display case, and handed it to Tiara. "On the house," she said. "Let's get busy and get this thing planned."

Forty-five minutes later, Holly's head spun with the overload of information. They planned a menu with drinks from an outside company and everything else catered by Holly. Tiara walked through the space, spouting orders, explaining how she wanted it to look the night of the party. It was going to require a lot of work and manpower. Manpower Holly didn't have. Thank God Tiara offered to bring in some outside help.

Tiara left her with a list of stuff to take care of before their next meeting, including a menu of what she planned to bake and what she was going to do with her inventory during the party. Tiara liked the idea of keeping her inventory front and center, of showing the public her quirky sense of style and the interesting concept of her business. She kissed the air on either side of Holly's cheek and breezed out the door.

Overwhelmed, Holly leaned against the counter and rubbed her forehead. Once again, she was in over her head. She was ruing the day Caleb had walked into her shop.

Caleb Peters. Gorgeous actor and pain in my ass.

Chapter Twelve

CALEB

Holly didn't return his text. After what happened with Anne Marie, he couldn't blame her.

"So what do you think?"

Caleb tucked his phone under his leg, shifted in his seat, and tapped his fork against his plate. "I'm sorry, what?"

Anne Marie sighed and rubbed her forehead. "I asked you if you thought we should get back together. I think it would be good for both of us. I mean, the press coverage alone would be great."

He snorted. "I don't want a girlfriend because I'll get good press coverage out of it."

Anne Marie rolled her eyes. "Do you think that's why I want a boyfriend? No, of course not. But when we're together, we both get great press. You know we do. I think we should reconcile. The gossip rags would eat it up." She put her hand on his. "And we're *good* together. I mean, the chemistry between us is phenomenal. And so is the sex."

Caleb's stomach clenched uncomfortably. He cleared his throat, opened his mouth, and snapped it shut again.

I don't think we were in the same relationship.

"Your enthusiasm is overwhelming." Anne Marie tossed her napkin on the table and slumped in her seat. "What's your deal, Caleb? Am I that repulsive?"

"What? No!" Leave it to her to twist things around and make him out to be a jerk.

The whole thing went downhill fast. He could see the headlines already. *Devastated Anne Marie Dumped by Caleb Peters. Again.* He'd come out of the first breakup unscathed. They both had. He wasn't sure that would happen again.

"Don't be ridiculous, Anne Marie. You're not repulsive, and you know it."

"Then what is it?"

It was his turn to rub his forehead. "I think..." He sucked in a deep breath and blew it out slowly before he responded. "I think we want different things."

"What is that supposed to mean?"

Caleb sighed. "Why do you want a relationship with me, Anne Marie? Is it for the publicity?"

Anne Marie rolled her eyes. "I don't know. Because we have fun? Because we look good together? Why does it matter? We date, we have sex, we get great press. We're both happy."

"I don't think that will make me happy."

Her eyes narrowed, and her mouth twisted in an ugly line. "I don't make you happy. Is that what you're saying?"

"No. I'm saying I don't know exactly what I want right now. But I do know I don't want a relationship where we each want something different. I don't want a relationship based on sex. I don't want to use my relationship to get press coverage. I don't think you want what I want."

She shoved her chair back and threw her napkin on the table. "You bet your ass I don't." She spun around, her cowboy boots slipping on the hardwood floor. She grabbed the back of the chair to catch herself, shot a dirty look in his direction, and stormed out of the room.

Caleb waved the waiter over and paid the bill. He texted Alex and told him he was going back up to his room. He checked his phone, hoping Holly answered his text, but there was nothing.

She could ignore him, but he wasn't giving up. He would call and text until she answered.

After three days, he gave up. The hit to his ego was too much. He'd called, texted, and left voicemail after voicemail, but Holly wouldn't answer him or return any of his calls. He finally called The Bookish Bakery and got Zoe on the phone.

"She can't come to the phone," Zoe said. "She said she's busy."

Caleb grunted. "Can you ask her to call me back? I really need to talk to her."

"I'll tell her, Caleb, but I don't think she'll call you back. I don't know what you did, but she's pretty upset."

He begged Zoe to give her the message one more time and hung up. His phone was still in his hand when it rang. Thinking Zoe had convinced Holly to call him back, he answered it without looking at the screen.

"Holly?"

"Caleb? What the hell happened with Anne Marie?"

"Hello to you, too, Paul. What do you mean, what happened with Anne Marie? Is there something online?"

"No. Not that I saw. Alex told me you guys had lunch and she left in a tiff. What happened?"

Caleb chuckled drily. "She wanted to get back together. I said no. She didn't like it."

Paul was quiet for a second before he said, "Okay."

"That's it? Okay? You aren't going to argue with me or tell me it would be good for my career to go out with Anne Marie?"

Paul burst out laughing. "Oh, hell no. I learned my lesson with Chris. I don't tell anyone who they should or shouldn't date." He cleared his throat. "I wanted to ask you about seeing the venue for the party. Is that something we can do?"

Shit.

"Um, yeah, sure," Caleb said.

"Great. I'm free tomorrow. I'll call Holly and arrange a time. I'll let you know." Paul disconnected the call.

Caleb exhaled and scrubbed a hand over the back of his neck. Tomorrow, he would see Holly. At least it would force her to talk to him. She couldn't completely ignore him if he was in the store.

This should be fun.

Alex held the door open and ushered them inside. He planted himself by the front door, attempting to look like he was browsing the bookshelves and not watching for stray paparazzi on the street. Tiny stood by the door as well, where he stuck out like a sore thumb.

"You two suck at blending in," Caleb whispered as he walked past his brother.

"Piss off," Alex growled. "Tiny, stay with Caleb."

Caleb chuckled and followed Paul into the store. Holly stood behind the display counter, and Zoe was in her usual spot behind the register.

Caleb pointed at Holly. "That's the owner right there."

Paul strode right up to her without hesitation and held out his hand. "How do you do, Ms. Wright? I'm Paul Tucker, Caleb's agent."

A sour look crossed Holly's face. She glanced at Caleb behind Paul. She straightened her shoulders and shook Paul's hand.

"Please, call me Holly."

"Holly it is." Paul glanced around the store. "I was hoping to look around the store if you don't mind. I wanted to get a feel for the place before the party."

Holly smiled and nodded. "Go right ahead. Would you like a cup of coffee?"

"That would be fantastic. I haven't had my caffeine yet today. I take it black." Paul turned to him. "Caleb? You want a cup?"

He gave Holly a hopeful grin. "I'd love a cup of coffee."

"Zoe! Can you get Mr. Peters a cup of coffee while I show Mr. Tucker around?" She poured coffee into a large to-go cup, stepped out from behind the counter, and handed it to Paul. "Let me show you what Tiara and I have been discussing."

She walked past Caleb without looking at him, gesturing for Paul to follow her. They vanished down the romance aisle, leaving Caleb standing at the counter alone.

"Do you take anything in your coffee?" Zoe asked.

"Cream and two sugars." He took off his sunglasses, tucked them in the front of his shirt, and adjusted his hat. "She's still mad at me?"

"I think so," Zoe replied. "Sorry."

"I deserve it. I was an ass."

Zoe pushed his coffee across the counter. "Do you mind if I ask what happened?"

"Like I said, I was an ass." He sipped his coffee. "Do you think I should apologize again?"

Zoe tipped her head to one side and made a weird face. "You apologized?"

"Yeah. Repeatedly. I mean, it was via text and voicemail, but that's only because she won't answer when I call." He shrugged. "I don't know what else to do, Zoe."

"Stop doing stupid shit," Alex interjected.

Caleb rolled his eyes and shook his head. "I'm trying. I screwed up. I know I screwed up. I knew it the second I did it. I wish I could rewind and do it again because, trust me, I would do all of it differently. Unfortunately, I can't. All I can do is tell her I'm sorry."

The shop door opened, and Tiara came in. She stopped and said hello to Alex, then she bounded up the stairs and slid to a stop in front of Caleb.

"Hi! Where's Holly?"

Caleb pointed over his shoulder. "She's showing Paul around."

"Perfect." Tiara spun around and darted down the romance aisle.

Caleb sat at a table in the café area near the display case. He propped his head on his hand and stared into space.

Zoe wandered over and set a piece of pastry in front of him. "Try this. It might cheer you up. It's my favorite."

"What is it?"

"An apple strudel. Holly makes the best I've ever had." She leaned over and tapped the table. "Compliment her on it. It will make her smile."

"Even if the compliment comes from me?"

"I hope so." She squeezed Caleb's shoulder. "Hey, does that big guy drink coffee?" She nodded Tiny's direction.

Caleb chuckled. "You'll make a friend for life if you take him a large black coffee and a sugar cookie."

Zoe laughed and winked at him. "On it."

Caleb closed his eyes and rested his head against the wall. Holly was angrier than he'd thought, and he wasn't sure he could make it up to her. Maybe it was for the best.

"This place is perfect," he heard Paul say.

As the three of them came around the corner, Caleb jumped to his feet and darted down the stairs. He stood behind them while Tiara pointed out several adjustments she planned to make, and Holly nodded along.

"It has amazing potential," Tiara said. "Holly and I have big plans. I can't wait for everyone to see it."

"Thanks so much for showing me around," Paul said. "I'm excited to see the place once it's all set up."

"It's going to be wonderful," Holly said. She took two steps back and bumped right into Caleb. He put his hand on the small of her back to keep her from falling. She grunted in surprise and swung around, a scowl marring her pretty face.

"Sorry," he mumbled.

"My bad," she said at the same time. She cleared her throat. "You didn't come with us on the tour."

"No, I didn't. I … uh … I want to be surprised. I know you and Tiara will do a wonderful job. You don't need my input to make it perfect. You've got it, I'm sure."

Tiara laughed. "Sweet talker." She turned to Paul. "I'll talk to you soon. Have a good day, everyone." She blew kisses to everyone as she walked out the door.

"If you'll excuse me, I have a cake to get in the oven," Holly said. "Mr. Tucker, it was nice to meet you." She took a deep breath and smiled at Caleb. "It was nice to see you, Caleb."

The smile didn't reach her eyes. He grabbed her hand before she could walk away.

"Holly? Can I have a word?"

She shook her head. "I don't think so. I have a lot of work to do. Goodbye, everyone." She yanked her hand out of Caleb's and disappeared through the swinging door leading to the kitchen.

He considered following her, but Paul was talking, and Alex was pushing him toward the door. As they left, Caleb looked over his shoulder. Holly stood in the doorway to the kitchen, watching them go.

Chapter Thirteen

HOLLY

Holly sipped her water and pushed away from her desk. Her eyes burned and her head pounded. It was the fifth night in a row she'd worked late.

Party planning was in full swing. Holly talked with Tiara daily, going over every little thing. The woman believed in preparing for every contingency. They had an alternate menu, an alternate party day should any issues arise, plans for rain, for sun, and for everything else in between. Every day closer to the party meant added stress for Holly.

On top of the party, business in the shop had picked up a lot. Thanks to Caleb's Instagram post when they'd first met, she had an influx of new customers. While some of those customers were nothing more than what Zoe called "looky-lous," some of them had become steady customers. A local book club adopted the shop as their meeting place, coming in every Tuesday morning for coffee, muffins, and a robust book discussion. Several of the people who came in to see where Caleb Peters got his book repeatedly came back, turning into regulars. Orders for custom cakes, cookies, and pies started coming in. Things were going so well Holly considered bringing in additional help.

Things were good. Holly should have been happy. But something kept her from completely enjoying her sudden prosperity.

Caleb.

Some days she wanted to forget Caleb existed, and some days he was all she could think about. The man had gotten under her skin, and she couldn't get him out. It was hard to pretend she wasn't interested in him when her world revolved around his wants and needs.

Thankfully, she didn't have to talk to him. Tiara was the liaison between the two of them; she knew what Caleb wanted and how far Holly would go to make it happen. All communication went through Tiara. Holly and Caleb hadn't talked in two weeks.

But just because she wasn't talking to him didn't mean she wasn't thinking about him. He was constantly on her mind. She replayed every conversation, every little thing they'd ever said and done, wondering if she had screwed it up.

Not that there was anything to screw up. She and Caleb went on two dates and kissed twice. It wasn't a relationship; it was barely the *beginning* of a relationship. Holly knew she was sending mixed messages, but so was Caleb.

She let her feelings get hurt, and she lashed out. Instead of giving Caleb a chance to explain why Anne Marie was in his hotel room, she got angry and blew him off. Fixing it seemed impossible; too much timed had passed. He probably didn't want to talk to her after two weeks of silence.

Holly checked her watch then shut her laptop. Zoe had gone home three hours ago, after Holly waved off her offer to grab drinks. Constant party planning and worrying over finances had her exhausted. She wanted to go to bed and sleep. Thank God the shop closed early on Sundays. She was going to turn off her phone, put on her favorite pajamas, and read a book until she fell asleep.

She grabbed her book from behind the register and headed up the stairs. She was halfway to her apartment when she heard a quiet tap on the back door. She considered ignoring it, but a delivery for Caleb's party was due any day. She set her book on the stairs and peered out the window.

The man standing at the door had a tattered backpack slung over his shoulder and wore an oversized leather jacket, sunglasses, and a baseball cap pulled down low. Between the sunglasses and the hat, Holly couldn't make out his face.

Who wears sunglasses at nine o'clock at night?

"Can I help you?" she called.

"Holly? It's me, Caleb. Can I come in?"

"Caleb?" She threw the lock and yanked open the door. "What... what are you doing here?"

He pulled the sunglasses off and looked up at her with red-rimmed, puffy eyes. If she had to guess, he hadn't slept for days. He shrugged and gnawed on his lower lip.

"I don't have any place to go," he mumbled. "The press surrounded my parents' house and my hotel. Alex said he even saw a couple of paparazzi outside of his and Miranda's place."

"What are you talking about? Why is the press at your parents' house? What is going on?"

"I'll explain everything, I swear." He glanced over his shoulder and shifted from foot to foot. "Can I come in?"

Holly stepped aside and let Caleb in. "Um, yeah, I guess."

He followed her upstairs to her apartment. Once they were inside with the door closed, Caleb tossed his backpack on the couch, along with his jacket and hat. He tucked the sunglasses in the pocket of his shirt. He dropped to the couch and put his head in his hands.

She leaned against the kitchen counter, crossed her arms over her chest, and stared at Caleb. "Tell me what's going on."

"You haven't seen it?" He pulled out his phone, tapped the screen a few times, and held it out to her. "It's everywhere."

Holly took the phone. The headline screamed at her from the screen.

Caleb Peters, Alcoholic!

The title took up the entire top of the page, bright, bold, gigantic letters screaming out something never meant to be made public. Below the headline was a terrible picture of Caleb; he had a bottle in his hand, a look of irritation marring his perfect face. He had one hand up, blocking the camera. He looked drunk.

Holly set his phone on the table and cleared her throat. "Is it true?" she asked.

"They left out the word 'recovering,'" Caleb said. "I'm a *recovering* alcoholic. I haven't had a drink since I was in my early twenties. But yes, Holly, I'm an alcoholic. When I was young, stupid, and making more money than I knew what to do with, all I wanted to do was party. Party and drink. Eventually, my drinking got out of control, and before I knew it, I couldn't start my day without a drink, couldn't memorize my lines without a drink, couldn't walk on set without a drink, and I couldn't sleep without a drink. I couldn't fucking do *anything* without a drink. On my twenty-third birthday, I went to a crappy dive bar to celebrate. I got into a fight and beat the shit out of this guy. I broke his nose and fractured his jaw. I don't even remember why he wanted to pick a fight with me. He sued, of course. I had just started a movie, and it was the best part I'd ever had. But the studio fired me because they thought there might be adverse publicity. Paul kept it out of the press, and Alex got me into rehab. I haven't had a drink since."

"This all happened, what, six years ago?" Holly asked. "Why is it coming out now?"

Caleb snorted and fell back against the couch. He put his arm over his eyes. "Read the story. Look at their source."

Holly scrolled through the story, skimming it. When she read the name of the source, she audibly gasped. "Anne Marie? I thought you two were together."

Caleb scoffed. "Together? Please. She was only with me for the publicity. This was a way for her to get attention. I never once drank alcohol when I was with her. We never got into a fight because I was drunk. I never, ever, used hardcore drugs, not before we were together or while we were together. Everything she said in that article about our relationship is a lie. She took something I told her in confidence, a truth I trusted her to keep to herself, and she told the world, twisting it to her advantage."

Holly frowned. "Is it really that bad? Maybe you're overreacting."

Caleb shot to his feet and paced the floor in front of the couch as he spoke. "The press is having a heyday. They're pulling out all the stops, overanalyzing everything I've ever done. Was he drunk here? Did he slur his words there? Why are his eyes bloodshot in that interview? Did he stumble because he was drunk? They are doing whatever they can to prove I'm still drinking." He pushed both hands through his hair, making it stand on end. "They're relentless, camped out at my parents' place, at Alex's, even following me from the hotel. Tiny drove like a damn maniac to get away from them. I slipped out of the car at a stoplight and snuck away like a common criminal."

"And you came here?"

"I'm sorry. I had nowhere to go. Once I was out of the car, I started walking, and before I knew it, I was standing at the end of the alley. I almost kept walking, but I wanted to…" He swallowed.

"I wanted to apologize. I'm sorry about everything. I'm sorry for showing up here unannounced, and I'm especially sorry about what happened at the hotel. I never should have let Anne Marie talk to you like that."

Caleb didn't look at her; he stared at his feet. Holly watched him pace the floor for almost a minute, the defeat on his face making her heart ache.

"You can stay here as long as you need to," she finally said. "In fact, I was about to make some dinner. I think I have enough for both of us. Are you hungry?"

"I'm starving. Absolutely starving."

Chapter Fourteen

CALEB

Relief flooded him when Holly asked if he was hungry. Maybe he wasn't completely forgiven, but she wouldn't kick him out when he was at his lowest point.

Holly made food—leftover pizza and a salad—and talked about anything but the tabloid headlines. He appreciated her efforts.

After they ate, Caleb offered to wash the dishes, and Holly let him. She excused herself, and he heard the shower come on. Fifteen minutes later, she emerged from the bathroom. His heart raced at the sight of her. Only she could make plaid pajama pants, a Bookish Bakery t-shirt, and a messy bun look so cute.

"Would you like to take a shower?" she asked. "I don't know if you have a change of clothes..."

He chuckled. "I've got sweats, clean socks, and underwear in my backpack. And yes, I would love a shower."

Holly smiled. "I thought you might. I left clean towels on the counter. I had an extra toothbrush, too."

"You're a saint. I'll just, uh..." He pointed over his shoulder at the bathroom door, snatched his backpack off the floor, and ducked into the bathroom. "Thanks again," he said before he closed the door.

When he came out, Holly had opened the sofa into a bed and made it. She'd also thrown some blankets and a pillow on the floor next to the small coffee table. She sat cross-legged on the floor with a book in her hand.

Caleb nudged her leg with his foot. "I won't take your bed. I'll sleep on the floor."

"You're my guest," she said. "You take the bed, and I'll sleep on the floor."

Caleb frowned. "I'm an unwanted guest who barged in on you unannounced. Let me sleep on the floor. I've imposed on you enough for one night."

Holly huffed, but she got to her feet, snatched the pillow off the floor, and threw herself on the sofa bed. She tossed a different pillow on the floor before she settled down in the center of the bed. She opened her book, propped it on her chest, and continued to read.

Caleb picked up his phone, but he wasn't interested in looking at anything on it, so he turned it off and set it on the table. He laid down, folded his hands on his stomach, and stared at the ceiling. Despite his exhaustion, he didn't think he would sleep.

Two hours later, he opened his eyes to a dark room, the only light from the streetlights outside. He had a lightweight blanket thrown over his legs. He didn't remember falling asleep or covering himself up. Holly must have done it.

He glanced at her, but all he could see was a bump under the covers. He sat up, drawing his knees to his chest like he'd done when he was a kid, and rested his chin on his knee. Every mistake he'd made the last few weeks played on repeat in his head.

He liked this woman. How did he let it get so bad, so fast?

Holly shifted beneath the covers and sighed.

Caleb rose to his feet and glanced at Holly. Her eyes were closed, and her breathing even. He went into the small kitchen and took a glass from the dish drainer. He filled it with water and stood at the sink, drinking it.

"Caleb?"

He swung around. "I'm sorry. Did I wake you?"

She sat up, propped on her elbows, her bun askew, and the light shining on her face, illuminating her beauty. She smiled and shook her head. "I wasn't asleep. Are you okay?"

He snorted. "Not really. I'm a piece of shit, Holly. I've treated you so… so shabbily, yet here you are, taking me in without argument. You could have turned me away, slammed the door in my face. But you didn't."

Holly climbed out of the bed and padded across the room to stand in front of him. "I'd like to think I'm your friend, Caleb. Friends don't turn their friends away when they're in need."

"You're amazing," Caleb whispered. "I don't deserve a friend like you."

Holly shrugged. "Well, you're stuck with me now." She giggled and held her hand out to him. "You should lie down. I'm sure you're exhausted after everything you've been through. A couple of hours of sleep isn't enough."

Caleb took her hand and let her lead him back across the room. They stopped next to the bed.

"Are you sure you don't want to sleep in the bed?"

Caleb shook his head. He closed his eyes and dragged in a deep breath. Holly smelled like honeysuckle and jasmine, the scent intoxicating. He reached for her, cupped her face in both hands, and kissed her. Then he rested his forehead against hers and caressed her cheeks with his thumbs.

"I'm sorry," he whispered.

"Don't apologize." She wrapped her arms around his waist and tugged him down onto the bed with her. "Just kiss me again."

Caleb laid down beside her and pulled her against his chest. She was warm and soft, impossible to resist. She traced her fingers over his t-shirt, tipped her head back, and pressed a kiss to his neck.

He swallowed a moan as she pushed her hands beneath his shirt and splayed her fingers across his back. She kissed his neck, his jaw, then her tongue drifted across his lips. His grip on her tightened, tugging her closer, the need to get her closer overwhelming him. His tongue slipped into her mouth, drawing her into a deep, soul-scorching kiss that made him ache with need.

Holly grabbed his wrist and pulled his hand up the side to her breast. Her back arched, silently encouraging him to touch her. His thumb brushed her nipple, the peak immediately hardening. She fisted his shirt in her hands and yanked it over his head, then she pulled off her own t-shirt and her pajama pants, followed by Caleb's sweatpants.

Caleb pulled her leg over his, his hardening cock pressing against her warm center through his boxers. He slid his hand up her thigh, cupped her ass, and pushed his hips up and into her.

Holly gasped his name and pulled him closer. Caleb eased his hand past the waistband of her panties, a deep growl leaving him. A shudder vibrated through her as he slowly caressed her. He ducked his head and wrapped his lips around her nipple.

She moaned and pushed herself down on Caleb's questing fingers. His cock ached, rock hard and trapped between their bodies. His groans matched Holly's as he rubbed against her. His teeth clamped down on her nipple, and she came, her hips rocking erratically.

Caleb shoved her panties down her legs, then he kicked off his boxers. He continued kissing her as they laid side by side, her leg thrown over his hip. He took his cock in his hand and lined it up with Holly's entrance. He stopped just before he entered her, his eyes locked on her bright hazel ones.

"Shit. I don't suppose you have a condom, do you?"

Holly squinted, and her brow furrowed. "Give me a second." She disentangled herself and skipped to the bathroom. She came back a few seconds later with a condom in her hand. "My ex left a bunch in the bathroom."

Caleb didn't want to ask about her ex, didn't even want to think about her being with anyone else. He grabbed her hand and dragged her back into bed. She giggled and fell on top of him.

"Is this okay?" he asked.

"Hell yeah," she whispered. "It's definitely okay."

Caleb slid the condom down his length, then he eased into her. He took his time, allowing her time to adjust to his size. Once he was inside, he wrapped both arms around her and moved his hips in slow, tight circles.

The insane intensity of sex with Holly was almost too much to handle. He forced himself to concentrate, to draw out the inevitable. He wanted to stay buried in Holly's warmth for an eternity, safe in her arms. His lips and hands were everywhere. Every tip of his hips pushed him deeper into her welcoming heat. She clung to him, her nails digging into his shoulders as they moved.

Caleb slid his hands up her back and gripped her shoulders. He pulled her down onto his thrusting cock, his hips pumped hard, the rhythm stuttering as he approached his release. Holly's walls tightened around him as she came again, drawing his own orgasm from him. He buried his face against the side of her neck as he climaxed, grunting as pleasure washed over him.

They separated, collapsing onto the small bed, shoulder to shoulder, hands clasped. Caleb closed his eyes and listened to Holly breathe, the sound lulling him to sleep.

Chapter Fifteen

HOLLY

Holly laid awake after Caleb fell asleep. She rolled over and snuggled up against Caleb's side. He sighed in his sleep and shifted closer to her.

She brushed her fingers up and down his arm, rested her forehead against his shoulder, and closed her eyes. Sleep came swiftly.

What seemed like a moment later, Holly's cell phone beeped incessantly from the other side of the room. She pushed Caleb's arm off and went to grab it off the kitchen counter. She hit the snooze button and dropped it back on the counter. She pushed her hands through her hair and sighed. Time to make the goodies.

"What time is it?" Caleb mumbled from the bed.

Holly tiptoed back to the bed and slipped in beside him. "It's five a.m."

Caleb opened one eye and looked at her. "Are you serious? No one gets up that early."

She giggled. "I have a lot of baking to do."

He wrapped her in his arms and nuzzled her neck. "You could stay here with me."

"As tempting as that is, I really have to get up. I have a special-order cake to make, and Tiara is coming by later to discuss the menu. I need to make her a few samples."

He propped himself on one elbow and looked down at her. "Shouldn't I be the one sampling stuff? It's my party."

"Um... well..."

"You didn't want me to come around, did you?"

"Caleb—"

He stopped her with a kiss, pressing his lips hard against hers. "It's okay. I get it. I was kind of an ass."

"I'm sorry."

"Don't be. I deserve it." He kissed her forehead. "You go work. I have a script I can go through. I don't want to disrupt your life."

Holly rose to her knees. "I'll tell you what. I'm going to go make a tray of muffins. While they're cooking, I'll get the cake in the oven. I'll bring the muffins up when they're done. How's that sound?"

"It sounds amazing." He rolled over and pulled the sheet up to his chin.

"I thought you had a script to read?"

"Mm-hm," he hummed.

Holly threw on some clothes, brushed her teeth, pulled her hair into a ponytail, and headed downstairs. She stood in the middle of the dark kitchen and took a deep breath, centering herself. She pushed all thoughts of Caleb out of her head—difficult to do when she could smell him on her skin—and set to work.

She hummed as she worked, moving by rote memory. After she put the cake in the oven, she set a timer on her phone and grabbed the muffins off the counter. As she stood in the middle of the kitchen, the swinging door opened, and Caleb stepped inside.

"Hey, what's up?"

"Do you need any help?"

"I think I'm good. Why don't we head back upstairs and have some muffins for breakfast?"

Halfway up the stairs, Holly stopped. "Shoot. I forgot to grab the milk."

"I'll get it," Caleb said.

"It's in the fridge next to the door."

Caleb bounded down the stairs and through the swinging doors. Inside her apartment, Holly thought she heard a faint knock on the back door. She set the muffins down so she could go check. She was standing on the landing outside her apartment door when Caleb sprinted up the stairs and pushed past her.

"What's wrong?" She followed him back into the apartment.

"The fucking paparazzi are everywhere," he snapped. "Up and down the street, out front. Everywhere." His eyes darted around until they landed on his phone on the coffee table. He grabbed it and punched in a number.

"Hey, Alex, it's me. I'm at Holly's, and the goddamn press are everywhere. I need you here. ASAP." He disconnected and shoved the phone in his pocket.

Holly stepped closer, but Caleb took a step back, his hands coming up as is he was going to push her away. She froze.

"Caleb?" she whispered.

"How did they know I was here, Holly?" The words were low and quiet, his voice deeper than usual.

"I don't understand what you're trying to say."

"The press. How did they find me? The only people who knew I was here were you and Tiny. So, tell me, Holly, how the fuck did the press find me?"

"Are you...?" She tried to swallow around the lump rising in her throat. "Are you accusing me of telling them you're here?"

"Tiny didn't do it. He's my bodyguard and my friend."

"And I just slept with you!" Holly yelled.

Caleb snorted. "It wouldn't be the first time someone slept with me for the publicity. Maybe you saw an opportunity to get some more attention for your failing bakery and bookstore." His words were biting and laced with anger. "It would help you out of the financial slump you're in, wouldn't it?"

Holly stared at him, her mouth hanging open. She had no words.

Caleb's phone rang. He yanked it out of his pocket and answered it. He said something she didn't register with the blood pounding in her ears. He grabbed his backpack and strode past her. Holly heard him go down the stairs, the back door open, then voices screaming Caleb's name. The door closed and then blessed silence.

Holly's knees gave out, and she slid to the floor.

"It'll blow over," Tiara said. "Things like this always do. Pretty soon, some other celebrity will do something stupid or some scandal will surface, and Caleb Peters will be old news."

Holly sipped her coffee and stared at the countertop. "He was so mad at me," she whispered. "He refused to listen to me, refused to believe me when I said I had nothing to do with it."

Tiara patted Holly's hand. "He's temperamental, sweetie. Like every other celebrity on the planet. Caleb gets especially difficult when he feels like he's backed into a corner. He lashes out at whoever is closest to him. The shit he put Alex through when he was going through rehab would make your head spin. Try not to take it personally."

A loud guffaw left Holly. "Yeah, sure. He bit my head off and accused me of using him to get publicity for my failing bakery and bookstore. He hurt me, T."

"I know he did. And I'm sorry about that. I know my apology doesn't mean shit because Caleb should be the one to apologize. He screwed up a good thing."

"A potentially good thing," Holly corrected her. "It wasn't like we made any commitments."

"Trust me, sweetie, if Caleb slept with you, it wasn't on a whim. It meant something to him. Caleb doesn't do one-night stands. He's not that kind of guy."

Holly pushed herself off the stool, grabbed the coffeepot, and refilled her cup. Then she excused herself to check on the pie she had in the oven. She was grateful for Tiara. A tentative friendship sparked between them during the party planning, and it had only grown as they spent time together. Tiara knew Caleb, and she didn't hesitate to call him on his shit. It had been Tiara who reached out to Holly when the press revealed he'd been hiding out at her store. She had immediately come down to the store to talk.

There was less than a month until Caleb's party, and Holly was eager to get it over with, especially since the press had descended on The Bookish Bakery. After the paparazzi caught Caleb at her place three days ago, they had been out front nonstop. They hung out on the sidewalk, snapping pictures of her any time she passed the window. Once or twice, they'd been bold enough to come in, but Zoe shooed them away.

But it wasn't just the paparazzi. Curious people wandered in and out of the store, not buying anything, only there to see where Caleb Peters had been. The influx of fans hoping to glimpse Caleb annoyed her regular customers. Irritated and sick of the press, Holly hung out in the back of the store.

Holly put the pie on the counter to cool and slipped a sheet of cookies into the oven. Zoe poked her head through the door.

"Hey, Holl, is it okay if I take off?" she asked. "I've got a mid-term tomorrow, and I need to study."

Holly cringed. Zoe leaving meant she had to go to the front of the store and deal with customers. Or the press. Neither was appealing.

"Um, yeah, sure, go ahead." She set a timer on her phone for the cookies and followed Zoe out front. A couple dozen people wandered the aisles, picking up books and checking out the display case of goodies. Tiara kept a wary eye on them.

Zoe grabbed her bag from under the counter, hugged Holly, and disappeared down the back hallway. Holly brushed the flour off her shirt and made her way to the counter. Tiara followed her.

"I was going to take off, but I can stay if you want company," Tiara said.

"Thanks, T, but I'm good. We're only open for two more hours. I can't hide behind Zoe forever. Besides, this crowd looks tame. Nobody has a camera." She shrugged and forced a smile onto her face. "I'm sure you have better things to do than hang out with me."

Tiara scowled. "I enjoy hanging out with you. You're the best thing to come out of this job in ages. But I have some phone calls to make, a few finishing touches for Caleb's party."

Holly scrunched her face, a sour taste in her mouth. She didn't want to think about Caleb.

Tiara squeezed her upper arm. "Sorry. Are you sure you don't want me to stay?"

"Go, go," Holly insisted. "I'll be fine. Let me just duck in the back and get the cookies out of the oven. Make sure nobody walks out with a book or anything."

Once the cookies were out and she'd said goodbye to Tiara, she returned to her stool behind the counter. Normally, she would be on the floor, chatting with the customers and recommending books. Not tonight.

"Excuse me, miss?"

Holly looked up, and a sudden flash of light blinded her. She rocked back and forth on the stool, and for a split second, she thought she was okay. But then she over-corrected, causing the stool to slip, and she fell. She landed on her side, her left arm twisted awkwardly under her. The thud reverberated through her, rattling her teeth and brain. She sat on the floor, stunned, for a full minute before she dragged herself to her feet. Everyone in the store stood in silence, staring at her.

Brian Drain, the rat-faced guy from The Gossip Monger, stood at the door. He nodded at her and waved his camera. "Thanks for the photo, Ms. Wright." He opened the door and vanished into the crowd.

Holly swallowed back the tears threatening to fall. She wasn't sure how much more she could take.

Chapter Sixteen

CALEB

Two weeks.

It took two weeks for the crap to blow over. Caleb spent most of it hiding out at his hotel or at his parents' place. Paul crafted a statement regarding the alcohol and drug rumors, portraying Anne Marie as the vindictive ex-girlfriend she was. It didn't take long before other ex-boyfriends of the country superstar spoke out. Tales of lies and false rumors abounded. The press turned on Anne Marie, demanding answers.

Two weeks before his party, Anne Marie came out and admitted she "might have exaggerated" when she spoke about Caleb's alcohol use. It wasn't an apology, which pissed him off. Unfortunately, there wasn't anything he could do about it.

After putting his life on hold for weeks, things were finally moving in the right direction. His movie got a director, his house was ready to move into, and the Sexiest Man Alive announcement was less than a week away.

If only he could fix things with Holly.

"Earth to Caleb." Tiara glared at him.

"Sorry. What did you say?"

He was with Tiara, discussing his party. At least that was why they'd gotten together. Instead, they were talking about Holly.

"I asked if you've talked to her since you ran away from her place."

Caleb shook his head. "No. I don't know what to say."

"She's hurt, Caleb. Literally and figuratively."

"What do you mean, literally?"

Tiara sighed. "That guy from The Gossip Monger came into her shop. He snapped her picture, blinding her with the flash, and she fell. Her stool tipped over, and she landed on her arm. Wounded pride and wounded arm."

"Is it bad?"

"It's only a sprain, but she's in a brace. Holly doesn't complain much, but I know it makes it hard to bake. Zoe has said as much. But worse than her arm, all this shit hurt her feelings. You hurt her feelings."

Caleb scrubbed at the back of his neck. "I know. I know I hurt her feelings, and I know I was an asshole."

"You need to apologize."

"Don't you think I've tried? She won't answer my texts. When I call, she sends it straight to voicemail. I keep screwing things up, and I can't fix it. It's making me crazy."

"Stop screwing up," Tiara said. "And maybe, instead of texting and calling, try driving down there and telling her you're sorry in person. I think it would mean a lot more if you said it to her face. Don't you?"

Caleb nodded. "Yes. I know it as well as you do. But I haven't been able to go anywhere. Now that things have calmed down, I can go talk to her."

Tiara nodded. "Good. For God's sake, do it before the party. Please. Otherwise, it's going to be awkward as hell."

"Are you sure about this?" Tiny asked.

"No, but I'm going to do it anyway. Tiara gave me an earful. Told me I need to stop screwing around and apologize in person. She's right."

"The store closes in half an hour. You better get in there."

Caleb pulled his sweatshirt hood up and stepped out of the SUV. He waited until traffic cleared, ran across the street, and ducked into the store. The bell overhead rang, signaling his entrance. He didn't see either Zoe or Holly anywhere on the floor.

"I'll be right with you!" Holly yelled from the kitchen.

He walked across the store, eased onto a stool at the counter, pushed his hood off, and looked around the store. He hadn't been in it for a few weeks, and things looked different.

The pastry display case was almost empty, with only a few cookies and a small pie left inside. The store was in disarray. They had moved tables and displays around, haphazardly stacked boxes lay strewn about the floor, and the walls were bare. It looked nothing like the small shop he'd been in before.

The kitchen door flew open, and Holly stepped out. "Sorry to keep you waiting. What can I do for you?"

She froze when she saw Caleb. She reached out and grabbed the counter, squeezing it so hard Caleb could see her white knuckles. Her face paled, and she blinked rapidly. "Caleb. Hi."

"How are you?" he asked.

Holly shrugged and cleared her throat. "I've been better."

Stung, Caleb shifted on the stool. He cleared his throat. "I know that's because of me, and I hate it. I want to apologize."

"It's too late to apologize," she snapped. Then she closed her eyes and exhaled. "I'm sorry. That was rude."

"I deserve it."

Holly's eyes snapped open. "Damn right you do."

Caleb cleared his throat. "The place looks different." Maybe if he started over, he could get his apology out.

Her hazel eyes darted around. "That happens when you're throwing a party for a big star. Your world turns upside down."

This isn't going well.

He scrubbed a hand over his face then pushed it through his hair. "I'm sorry, Holly. I'm sorry about everything. I'm sorry I came into your life and turned it upside down. I can't apologize enough. Helping me wasn't supposed to be hard on you. I didn't want you to get hurt."

She snorted. "I did, though."

Caleb clasped his hands in front of him and leaned over the counter. "I know. I swear I do. That's on me. One hundred percent on me. I blamed you, and that was stupid. Can you ever forgive me?"

Holly crossed her arms over her chest and stared at her feet. "I can forgive you. Holding a grudge isn't in my nature."

"That's great, Holly—"

"I'm not finished," she interrupted. "I can forgive you, but that's as far as it goes. I can't live in your world, Caleb. I don't want to. It's too insane, too crazy. Anything that might have happened between us, it's over."

Caleb's heart stuttered. "Can't we talk about this?"

Holly shook her head. "I don't think there's anything to talk about."

"Okay," Caleb said. He eased off the stool. Suddenly, anger built in his chest like a volcano about to explode. "You know what? You're probably right. Our worlds are too different. *We're* too different. It was a mistake coming here."

He yanked his hood up, spun around, and stomped out the door. He barely registered the honking cars as he crossed the street without looking. He jerked the SUV door open.

"How'd it go?" Tiny asked.

"Take me home. Now." He slumped in his seat and hid his face against the window. For the first time in six years, he desperately wanted a drink.

Chapter Seventeen

HOLLY

"Holly?"

She swung around at the mention of her name, fumbling with the stack of books in her arms.

"Alex, hi." She forced a smile onto her face. "What are you doing here?"

"I thought Tiara told you I was coming by," he said.

Crap. I forgot.

Holly closed her eyes and nodded. "Yeah, yeah, she did. You're going to check security, right?"

Alex nodded and crossed his substantial arms over his chest. "I am. I need to check exits, look over the entrance, and see if there are any issues I need to address before the party."

"What do you need from me?"

"I need your permission to look around."

Holly set the stack of books on the counter and held her arms out. "Go wherever you need to go. Let me know if you need anything."

Holly and Zoe spent the next hour rearranging shelves and moving tables while Alex looked around the store, jotting notes on a small notepad he kept in his pocket.

"I'm all finished," he said. "If it's okay with you, Friday morning I'd like to bring my team by to let them look around and familiarize themselves with the layout. I'm a guest Saturday night, so I want them to know what they're getting into ahead of time."

"Sure, whatever you need to do." She bent to pick up a box, but it was too heavy thanks to her wounded arm. She kicked it across the floor but stopped when she heard Alex exhale loudly.

"Can I put that somewhere for you?" he asked.

"That would be great. It goes down there." She pointed to the other side of the room. "I need to put them on the shelves."

Alex hefted the box onto his shoulder like it weighed nothing, carried it across the room, and set it on the floor. He ripped it open like it was closed with Velcro and pulled out the books, handing them to Holly one by one.

Alex cleared his throat. "How have you been?"

She shrugged. "Okay, I guess."

Alex narrowed his eyes. "You know, you promised my family you wouldn't be a stranger. My parents ask about you all the time."

Holly laughed. "Well, things aren't exactly good between me and Caleb—"

Alex held up his hand, stopping her. "It's okay. You don't have to explain. I know how my brother is, and I know some of what happened between the two of you." He sighed and shook his head. "I'm meeting my parents for lunch up the street in half an hour. Will you join us?"

She shook her head. "Oh, I couldn't."

"My parents would love to see you. Please?"

"I'm not up to seeing Caleb."

"He won't be there. He and Tiny are at the studio. Caleb has a read-through for his new movie. It will just be me and my parents."

Holly considered arguing, but she didn't think it would do any good. Besides, if Caleb wouldn't be there, she didn't have a reason to say no. She genuinely liked Jack and Wendy; it would be good to see them.

"Okay, let me tell Zoe I'm going to lunch." She went to the back of the store, found Zoe, and told her about lunch. A ridiculous grin spread across her friend's face.

"Cool it, Zoe," she snapped. "This has nothing to do with Caleb. He won't even be there. His parents are nice people, and I like them. It's just lunch. I'll be back in an hour."

She and Alex left the store and walked down the street in silence. She wasn't sure what to say to him. He was intimidating.

"Do you want to talk about what happened with Caleb?" he asked.

"You mean you don't know?" Holly found that hard to believe.

"I only know what Caleb told me. He said it was a misunderstanding. I'd like to hear your side if you're all right with telling me."

Holly exhaled slowly and gnawed on her lower lip. "Caleb came to my place after the tabloids came out with the story about his drinking. He stayed the night with me, and the next day, the press was outside. He... he blamed it on me, accused me of telling them he was there to get publicity for my failing store. He said some not-so-nice things and stormed out."

Alex listened patiently, waiting until she finished before he spoke. "Okay. Well, first, my brother's an idiot. But in his defense, the paparazzi are relentless. He can't go anywhere or do anything without them hounding him. When the rehab stuff came out, it was especially hard on him. He worked for years to keep it a secret. He is ashamed of what happened and of how screwed up things got. He didn't trust anybody with that secret. I think, for a while, he thought Anne Marie might be the real thing. Obviously, that wasn't the case. It tore him apart when she tried to use his secret against him. I know it's asking a lot, but maybe you could give him a break."

Heat flooded her cheeks. She wondered if Alex knew Caleb had called and texted her too many times to count or that he'd come to the store and she'd sent him away. She'd did it to save her dignity, and she couldn't go back in time and change anything as much as she wanted to.

Alex held open the restaurant door for her and gestured for her to go in ahead of him. She spotted his parents right away. A smile spread across Wendy's face when she saw Holly. She and Jack rose to their feet as they approached.

"Holly!" Wendy hugged her tight. "It's so good to see you. This is a wonderful surprise."

Alex kissed his mother's cheek. "Hi, Mom. I was in Holly's shop, checking security for Saturday night, and I invited her to lunch."

"I hope you don't mind," Holly said.

"Of course, we don't mind," Jack said. He winked at her, pulled out a chair, and gestured for her to sit.

Conversation with Caleb's family was easy. They were some of the kindest people she knew. On the walk over, she'd worried things would be awkward because of Caleb, but it was like she was part of the family. Holly allowed herself to relax and enjoy the lunch.

Until Caleb entered the restaurant.

Holly stopped talking mid-sentence, her mouth snapping shut with a noticeable click. Alex's eyes widened as his brother approached the table. He glanced at Holly and mouthed "sorry."

Caleb didn't see her right away; he was engaged in conversation with Tiny. When his eyes finally locked with hers, he stopped dead in his tracks. Her heart pounded in her ears as they stared at each other over the table.

Caleb smiled first. "It's good to see you, Holly. How have you been?"

His formality hurt more than she imagined it would. Two could play that game. "I'm doing well. Thank you." She picked up her fork and pushed her salad around the plate, her ears tuned to the surrounding conversation. She didn't contribute. Every time she looked up, she caught Caleb staring at her.

Lunch with the Peters and Tiny turned out to be the longest forty-five minutes of her life. The server was clearing the plates away when Caleb slipped into the empty chair beside her. He put his arm on the back of the chair and leaned over.

"Hey," he murmured.

"Hi." Her smile felt like more of a grimace.

"Do you think we could talk?"

Holly sighed and shook her head. "I don't want to talk, Caleb. Please … let's get through lunch and go our separate ways. Okay?"

Caleb swallowed, dropped his arm, and shifted back in his seat. He sighed and nodded. "Okay. But let me say one thing. I am sorry about what happened. All of it. The shit with Anne Marie, the accusations I made, even my visit to the store the other night. I was an ass, and I've made a lot of horrible mistakes. I know there is no way I can make it up to you, but I'd like to try."

Holly shrugged. "I don't think we should talk now. Maybe later?"

"Thank you," Caleb whispered.

"I said maybe," Holly reiterated. "I'm not rushing into anything. We'll talk, and that's it. Okay?"

"Okay. Later it is."

Holly excused herself to use the restroom. She leaned against the door after she locked it and took a second to catch her breath. Then she splashed water on her face, checked her hair, and straightened her clothes. Once her heart stopped racing and the deep red blush on her cheeks turned a rosy pink, she opened the door and stepped into the hallway. As she passed the bar, she heard voices around the corner.

"No one can see me with her, Tiny."

It was Caleb. Holly stopped and stepped back into the shadows.

"If people see us together after what happened, they'll get the wrong idea. The press will eat her alive. Some no name bookstore owner dating a celebrity. How's that going to look? I can hear the bullshit already."

Holly bit her lower lip hard enough to draw blood. Hot tears stung the corners of her eyes. She darted past the bar, out the front door, and jogged up the street. She needed to put as much distance as possible between herself and Caleb Peters.

"Holly!" Zoe yelled from the front of the store. "There's someone here to see you."

Holly sighed and pushed through the kitchen door. It was too early for this. The store had only been open for ten minutes. Even though she wasn't in the mood for anyone, she would play the part. She was over everybody and everything.

It was two days until Caleb's party. Once it was over, she was closing for a week and hiding from the world. She needed to recharge and regroup, alone and without constant distractions.

She tightened the strings of her apron, put a smile on her face, and stepped onto the floor. Caleb stood next to the display case, a brown package in his hands. He shifted from foot to foot.

"Caleb? What are you doing here?"

"You disappeared yesterday," he replied. "I tried to call you—"

"I turned off my phone."

Caleb cleared his throat. "Why did you leave? I thought we were going to talk."

She could lie to him, fill his head with platitudes meant to make him feel better, but when she opened her mouth, that wasn't what came out. "I heard what you said to Tiny."

"What do you mean?"

"I believe you called me a 'no name bookstore owner.' Wasn't that what you said?"

The blood drained from his face, and he visibly swallowed. "Let me explain. I was trying to protect you—"

"No. I don't think I want to hear your excuses. See, Caleb, every time I let you in, I end up hurt while you come out of it unscathed. It's too much. *You're* too much. Caleb Peters, the movie star, is too much."

"You know none of that is real, right? The public persona, movie star Caleb. That isn't me. Who I am when I'm with you is the real me. Please give me a chance to prove to you I can be the man you want and need."

Her shoulders slumped. "I'm sorry, Caleb. I can't." She blinked rapidly, praying the tears prickling at the corner of her eyes wouldn't fall.

Caleb licked his lips and nodded. He set the package on the counter, patted it twice, and turned to leave. He opened the door, the bell ringing cheerily, but stopped with his hand on the knob and looked back at her.

"I'll see you Saturday night."

The door swung closed behind him.

"What's in the package?" Zoe asked.

Holly jumped. She didn't expect anyone to be behind her. She'd been staring at the brown package in her hand for the last ten minutes, her heart in her throat, silently weeping.

"I... I don't know." She swiped at the tears on her cheeks and sniffled.

"Why don't you open it?"

"I should give it back to Caleb. I just rejected him. I shouldn't keep it."

Zoe put an arm around Holly and rested her head on her friend's shoulder. "He obviously wants you to have it, or he wouldn't have left it. Open it, Holl."

Holly peeled back the paper. As soon as she saw what was inside, fresh tears spilled down her cheeks.

"It's a book," she choked out. "My favorite book." She flipped it open. "Jesus Christ, Zoe, it's signed. Do you know how rare this is?"

"He knew this was your favorite book?"

"I can't believe he remembered. We talked about it the first time he was in the store. I made some offhand comment about loving *Little Women* and Louisa May Alcott since I was a little girl. I told him that love spurred my love of all books. I didn't expect him to remember."

"Looks like he did." Zoe cleared her throat. "Was that why he stopped by? To give you a gift?"

Holly shrugged. "I don't know. I didn't give him a chance to tell me."

"You're kidding, right?"

"I know how it sounds, Zoe. I do. But Caleb Peters is a lot to take."

Zoe laughed. "Caleb Peters, the movie star, is a lot to take. What about Caleb? He seems like a pretty good guy."

A dull headache formed behind Holly's eyes. Her world had spun out of control, and she couldn't set it right. "I don't know what to do, Zoe. I honestly have no clue."

Zoe hugged her again. Holly clung to her friend and let the tears fall.

Chapter Eighteen

CALEB

"You look great," Miranda said. "But you need to smile."

Caleb straightened his tie and shrugged. "I'll smile when the cameras are pointed at me."

"Are you okay?"

Caleb looked at his sister-in-law. She looked beautiful in a pair of jeans, a black sequined top, and heels. The woman exuded elegance and confidence.

"How do you do it?"

Her brows furrowed, and she tipped her head to one side. "How do I do what?"

"How do you stay *you*? How come you don't have some magic persona you switch on when you go in front of the cameras? You're the same person sitting here talking to me that goes on Good Morning America and talks about her new movie."

Miranda leaned forward, her elbows on her knees. "I'm just me. I promised myself I wouldn't change who I was when I became an actor. If people don't like me—the real me—then they don't like me. Staying true to myself is more important than putting on some persona."

Caleb sighed and sat down. He rested his head against the back of the couch. "I don't know how to do that."

"Why not?"

"I don't think people would like who I really am. I was a bookworm growing up. A nerd. A goofball. I didn't get where I was because I was that guy. People love the reserved Caleb Peters, the Caleb Peters who is aloof and keeps things close to the chest. That Caleb is a mystery women want to unravel. The press and my fans like that guy."

"How do you know they won't like nerdy Caleb if you never let him free?" Miranda crossed the room and crouched in front of him. "I like *that* Caleb. He's fun and quirky and a great brother-in-law."

"Yeah, but is he the sexiest man alive?" Caleb asked.

"Yes, he is." Miranda pushed to her feet. "Be yourself, Caleb. Let the real you out. Set him free. You'll find your happiness. Trust me." She kissed the top of his head. "I'm going to go find Alex. I'll see you at the party."

Caleb put his head in his hands and took a deep breath. He sat on a precipice. He had a chance to change, to move forward, to get want and who he wanted. He exhaled and pushed to his feet.

Time to go.

Despite the event being billed as a private party, a large crowd of people gathered in front of The Bookish Bakery. Word had gotten out about the party—thanks to a well-timed press release from an anonymous source—and people came out in droves to see Caleb. They crowded against the velvet ropes lining the sidewalk and spilled into the street. Two hours earlier, People Magazine had announced him as their Sexiest Man Alive, hyping the crowd into a near frenzy.

Caleb peered out the car window. The outside of the store looked amazing. A red carpet led to the door and twinkling lights lined the large front window. A spotlight lit up an extra-large version of his Sexiest Man Alive issue in the center of the window display.

Tiny opened the back door of the SUV, and Caleb stepped out. People screamed his name from every direction. He smiled and waved at the crowd. He signed copies of his magazine and posed for selfies as he walked the red carpet to the door. Tiny stuck close, walking a few steps behind him, his eyes on the crowd.

CHAPTER EIGHTEEN

As soon as Caleb stepped inside the store and the door closed behind him, silence descended. It didn't last long, only a second, before everyone in the room burst into applause.

Holly had completely transformed the store. She'd draped twinkling lights along the railings in front of the register and display case and across the top of the shelves. The tables in the front now held food and drinks instead of books. Copies of his magazine graced the tables in the small cafe area near the entrance to the kitchen, and his movie posters replaced the book posters on the walls. Smartly dressed servers stood at the ready, drink and hors d'oeuvre trays in hand. Zoe stood behind the counter, dressed like the servers but also wearing her Bookish Bakery apron. Caleb didn't see Holly.

Tiara appeared at his side. "What do you think?"

"It looks fantastic," he said. "You and Holly did great, T. I was in here two days ago, and it didn't look anything like this. You really transformed this place."

"I couldn't have done it without Holly. She busted her butt to get it ready. Wait until you see all the things she made to eat. It's incredible."

Caleb followed Tiara through the crowd to the display case. A large table covered in every sweet treat imaginable stood in front of it. Cakes, cookies, pies, candy, crispy rice treats, fruit tarts, cupcakes, and cheesecakes. The amount of food overwhelmed him. He didn't know how Holly pulled it off. She was incredible.

"You should thank her," Tiara whispered.

Caleb nodded. "I plan on it. Do you know where she is?"

"Probably hiding in the back. She wants to stay out of the spotlight. You go mingle and say hi to everyone. I'll find Holly and see if I can coax her out here."

Caleb watched Tiara go into the kitchen, wondering if he should go with her. As if she read his mind, Tiara turned and waved at him to go. He'd give anything to spend the night talking to Holly instead of hanging out with his friends and family. But he wanted to have fun and enjoy tonight. He'd waited this long to talk to Holly, and he could wait a little longer. Or at least until Tiara gave him the okay.

"Caleb!" Miranda swooped in and wrapped her arms around him. "This place is amazing. I love it! Having your party here was a great idea. Where's Holly? I want to pick her brain about books. I could hang out here forever."

Caleb laughed. "She'd love that." He clapped Alex on the shoulder. "Have you tried any of the baked goods? Holly is hands down the best baker I've ever met. Her sweets are phenomenal."

Alex chuckled and patted his stomach. "I've tried several things, but the boss cut me off." He jutted a thumb in Miranda's direction.

Miranda giggled and poked her husband in the stomach. "Gotta keep you in shape so you can keep us safe," she teased.

Alex snorted. "Yeah, well, I'm going back over there to try those cookies. I saw snickerdoodles."

Miranda smirked. "Your favorite. Let's go." She took Alex's hand and let him lead her across the room. She waved at Caleb over her shoulder.

Caleb circled the room, stopping and talking to his friends and family. Once he'd come full circle, he made his way to where Zoe stood at the counter.

"Well, if it isn't the sexiest man alive," Zoe said and smiled at him. "How's it going, Caleb?"

"Not too bad. The place looks great. I can't tell you how much I appreciate it."

"You should thank Holly. This was all her doing. She didn't sleep last night. She stayed up decorating and baking."

"Seriously? She stayed up all night?"

Zoe leaned on the counter. "She wanted everything to be perfect."

"She succeeded."

"Do you know why she wanted it to be perfect?"

Caleb smiled. "I have a feeling you're going to tell me."

"She did it because she cares. She cares about this place. And she cares about you." Zoe straightened up. "I just thought you should know that."

Caleb nodded. "Thank you, Zoe," he whispered.

"She's in the kitchen. Go talk to her."

He didn't have time to find Holly, though, because Paul appeared out of nowhere, grabbed his arm, and dragged him up a short set of stairs to the large picture window at the front of the store. His manager tapped a spoon against his glass to get everyone's attention.

"Hey, everybody. I'd like to thank you for coming out to celebrate People Magazine's Sexiest Man Alive, Caleb Peters!"

The room broke out in applause, his friends and family hooting and hollering, a few playful heckles thrown in for good measure. Caleb laughed and shook his head.

"Let's see if we can't get the man of the hour to say a few words." Paul stepped to the side and pointed at Caleb.

Caleb chuckled as he stepped forward. He waited for the cheering to die down before he spoke.

"Thank you, everybody, for coming out. Who knew when I was a gangly teenager tripping over my own feet that, fifteen years later, I'd be People Magazine's Sexiest Man Alive?"

"Not me!" Alex shouted.

Caleb shook his head. "That makes two of us, bro."

"Three," Rylan interjected.

"My brothers, ladies and gentlemen. Always supportive." He exhaled. "But seriously, I never thought I would be here. I'm so grateful to everyone who helped me along the way. Alex for helping me get my first job; Mom and Dad for supporting me when I pursued acting; Rylan for all those nights staying up late, helping me learn my lines or following me around some movie set; and my manager, Paul, for taking a chance on a young kid. Without all these people in my life, I wouldn't be who I am." He raised his arms over his head. "People's Sexiest Man Alive!"

The room erupted in cheers again. Caleb grabbed a sparkling water off the nearest table and downed it in two swallows.

"Everybody have a great time!"

Out of the corner of his eye, he saw Holly duck back into the kitchen. He set his drink down and went after her.

Chapter Nineteen

HOLLY

It took her a ridiculous amount of time to pick out something to wear. It wasn't even her party; it shouldn't concern her if she looked good or not. She was there to serve her baked goods and smile at Caleb's guests.

Clothes covered the pullout sofa. Dresses, slacks, blouses, jeans, t-shirts, and everything imaginable. She'd tried on and rejected more than half the clothes in her closet.

Holly glanced at the clock. She pushed her hands through her hair and dropped to the edge of the couch. Her left eye twitched, and she couldn't stop sweating.

The thought of seeing Caleb or talking to him terrified her. She screwed up everything. She didn't expect her rejection of him to turn her world upside down. The depth of her feelings for the handsome actor surprised her. A thousand times over, she asked herself if she'd done the right thing. The answer was always no. No matter how many times she told herself it was to save her sanity, her heart still hurt.

Zoe poked her head through the door. "Tiara says Caleb is ten minutes out." She scrunched up her nose. "You're not ready." It was more an accusation than a statement.

Holly shrugged. "I can't decide what to wear."

Zoe strode into the room, snatched a pair of black pants and one of Holly's white Bookish Bakery shirts off the bed, and threw them at her.

"Wear that." She posed with one hand in her hair and her foot lifted slightly. "We'll match."

Holly gave her friend a weak smile. "Thanks." She rose to her feet with a weary sigh.

Zoe hugged her. "Fake it 'til you make it, sweetie. It will be okay."

Holly nodded. "I know."

Zoe turned to go but stopped short and swung around. "I swear this is the last time I'll say this. Talk to him. Tell him how you feel. He deserves to know."

"I already turned him down."

"Yeah, well, we're allowed to change our minds. *You're* allowed to change your mind."

"I don't know if it will do any good," Holly said.

"I know." Zoe smiled. "If it's meant to be, it's meant to be. Promise me you'll try."

"I'll think about it."

"That's all I ask. I'll see you downstairs."

Holly stood in the center of the room until the door closed behind Zoe. Then she tucked her clothes under her arm and took a deep breath. If the chance arose, she would talk to Caleb. Zoe wouldn't leave her alone if she didn't try. At least she would know once and for all how he felt about her.

Her hands shook, and the twitch in her eye was back. She couldn't wait for this night to be over.

She knew the second Caleb's car pulled up in front of the store. The crowd had been loud, the sound a constant hum in the background all afternoon. But when the clock hit seven p.m., the noise became indescribable. Screaming and shouts of his name filled the air. Holly wanted to be out there, standing beside Zoe and representing the store, but she wasn't sure she could bring herself to smile, not when her heart ached so bad. It was easier to stay out of the way, so she busied herself in the kitchen.

Thirty minutes later, Tiara burst through the door like her ass was on fire. "Holly! What are you doing back here? You need to be out front and center selling the business and hyping up your baked goods, not hiding in here."

"I'm checking—"

Tiara cut her off with a hand in her face. "Nope. There is nothing in here requiring your attention." She pointed at the empty ovens and the clean countertops. She turned her all-knowing eyes on Holly. "You're hiding from Caleb."

Holly rolled her eyes. "Yeah, so?"

"Go talk to him. I'm sure he wants to see you."

"I doubt it. Besides, I can't face him, T. Not after he came in here, put his heart on the line, and I refused to give him a chance. I'll stay in here and stay out of his way. Let him have his time in the spotlight."

Tiara scoffed. "Caleb's life is lived in the spotlight, Holl. Every minute of every day. He won't mind giving up a few minutes to talk to you. Trust me. Now, get your ass out there."

Holly sighed. "Okay, okay. Give me a few minutes and I'll be out."

Tiara pursed her lips, but she nodded. "If you're not out there in five minutes, I'm coming back." She shook her finger in her friend's face. "You do *not* want me to come back in here." She spun on her heel with a loud huff and left.

I can do this. I can go out there and act like everything is okay.

Holly pulled her apron on and tied it. Then she untied it and did it again. She yanked her ponytail out, ran her fingers through her hair to fluff it, pushed open the kitchen door, and stepped into the insanity of a Hollywood party.

Caleb stood at the front of the store with his manager. Paul got everyone's attention, then he introduced the man of the hour. Caleb smiled and stepped forward. His speech was brief and kind of sweet, exactly what she would expect from him. A part of her ached to be standing beside him or even have him mention her name. When everyone raised their glasses to drink, Holly ducked back into the kitchen.

I had to fall for the attractive actor, didn't I?

She picked up a rag and wiped down the spotless counter. She wanted to go out there and talk to him, start over, and see if they could get it right. Holly wracked her brain, trying to think of something, anything, to say to Caleb. Nothing seemed appropriate.

"Holly?"

She froze, her heart in her throat. The dishcloth fell to the counter as she turned around slowly. Caleb stood in the doorway, looking utterly gorgeous in his gray suit. His hair was perfectly messy, reminding her of how he looked when he first woke up in the morning. Her heart stuttered at the memory.

Caleb took a step closer to her, a tentative smile on his face. "Hey, Holly."

Holly returned the smile. "Hi, Caleb. How are you?"

"I'm doing well. I wanted to… I wanted to come in here and, uh, thank you. The store looks amazing. The food is amazing. Everything is…"

"Amazing?"

Caleb chuckled. "Yeah. Yeah, it's amazing. I'm sorry. I'm not so good at this stuff."

"Talking? You're not good at talking?" She giggled nervously. "Isn't that what you do for a living?"

Caleb shook his head. "I'm not good at talking to *you*, Holly. You fluster me, make me nervous. I can't seem to get the words out, not the *right* words anyway. Every time we talk, I stick my foot in my mouth."

Holly snorted. "Damn right you do."

"This is definitely not as easy as it is in my movies."

"Maybe you should try quoting one of them. You might not get tongue-tied if you use someone else's words."

Caleb inched closer, so close the spicy scent of his cologne assaulted her. She squeezed the edge of the counter, holding herself upright. She resisted the urge to jump into his arms and kiss him.

Caleb took another step closer. "There isn't anything that anyone has written that can express how I feel about you, Holly," he whispered.

"Wh-what?"

He stood right beside her. He placed his hand over hers and gently squeezed it. "I've said some of the most romantic lines ever written. I've made women swoon with words someone else put in my mouth. None of those words are good enough for you. None of them come close to explaining the depth of my feelings for you."

"Caleb—"

"I'm serious. I get tongue-tied around you because I know whatever I say won't be good enough. I desperately want to tell you how I feel, how you make me feel. Instead, I open my mouth and say something stupid."

"It's not all stupid," Holly said. "That was pretty good."

Caleb laughed. "Yeah? I thought I did okay."

"So, now that you have my attention, is there something you want to say?"

Caleb cupped her cheek and brushed a kiss across her lips. He twisted a strand of her hair around his finger as he stared into her eyes. Her insides twisted, and heat rushed through her.

A smile spread across his face. "Excuse me, miss. Can you help me find a book?"

Chapter Twenty

CALEB

One Month Later

Caleb shifted in his seat and stared out the window at the crowd lining the street. The turnout was insane, far more than he'd thought. His name in the press repeatedly over the last month had fueled the anticipation for the new movie. Not to mention that the critics loved it. Talk of another Academy Award nomination was everywhere. He tried not to think about it; if he did, he would puke.

"Are you ready?" he asked.

Holly squeezed his hand, but she didn't answer him. He turned to look at her.

She was ghost white, her red lipstick harsh against her pale face. The hand he held shook uncontrollably, and her eyes were glassy.

He brushed a strand of hair off her face and leaned over her. "Baby? Are you okay?"

"I—" She visibly swallowed, closed her eyes, and exhaled. "I'm sorry. I'm really nervous."

Caleb scooted closer and wrapped his arm around her waist. "Of course, you are. This is scary. Five minutes before I walked the red carpet for the first time, I puked in the bathroom. Paul met me in the hallway outside the restrooms with a package of mints."

"Oh god, I hope I don't puke." She shook her head and sucked in a deep breath.

"It's okay. You'll be fine."

"Easy for you to say. Everybody in the world is judging me, watching and waiting for me to make a mistake. Anything to scream about my extreme unworthiness. Your fans don't like me, Caleb. They're waiting for me to make some kind of unforgivable blunder so they can tear me to shreds."

Caleb cupped her cheeks in his hands. He pressed his forehead to hers. "You are not unworthy," he whispered. "I don't deserve you. I don't care what the rest of the world thinks. I don't care what my so-called 'fans' think. They don't matter. You are perfect. If they don't like you, they aren't a genuine fan. They should be happy that you make me happy."

Holly smiled, and a hint of color touched her cheeks. "Thank you. Have I told you I love you?"

"Yes, but I enjoy hearing it again." He gently kissed her. "Come on, let's go watch my movie."

The limousine door opened. Caleb stepped out, turned, and held out his hand. Holly took it and climbed out of the car. She looked stunning in a royal blue off-the-shoulder dress, her honey-blonde hair falling down her back in soft waves. She put a smile on her face and squared her shoulders.

He couldn't resist; he leaned down and kissed her again. She stared up at him, her hazel eyes sparkling with unshed tears.

"Are you sure you're okay?" he asked.

Holly nodded. "As long as I'm with you, I'm fine." She stared at the screaming crowd. "You'll tell me if I do anything wrong, right?"

"I won't have to, baby. You're perfect. Now, smile big and wave at the fans."

Holly took his arm and put a smile on her face. Caleb couldn't be prouder of her.

Despite the intense scrutiny and stress put on her because she was dating him, she kept a smile on her face. Business was booming, thanks in part to his party and because of her newfound and sudden infamy as Caleb Peters' girlfriend. She persevered, doing her best not to let his fans and the gossip sites get to her.

"Caleb?" Holly poked him in the side.

"Hm? What?"

Holly pointed at the crowd. "Smile big and wave at the fans, sweetheart."

Caleb laughed, pulled her into his arms, and lifted her off her feet. He kissed her with a loud smack. The crowd cheered.

"See? They love you," he said.

She giggled. "Only because you do." She kissed his cheek. "Come on, let's go find that Gossip Monger guy and rub this in his face."

Caleb snorted. "That's my girl."

Other Books by Mimi Francis:

No Choice

Unwrap Me: An XXX-mas Anthology
Stuffing My Socking: An XXX-mas Anthology
My Wedding Date Anthology

Private Lives
Private Protection
Priavte Party
Private Desires

Run Away Home
The Professor
Out Two-Week, One-Night Stand
Can't Fight the Feelings
Lakeside Love: The Collection - Books 1-3

Taken by the Mobster

The Sugar Daddy Arrangement

Book Club Questions

1. Holly's bookstore/bakery is a creative and cozy setting for the story. How does her business reflect her personality? What do you think makes bookshops and bakeries such appealing settings in romance novels?
2. Caleb Peters is the ultimate celebrity heartthrob, but he struggles with the pressures of fame, particularly the lack of privacy. How do you think his celebrity status influences his relationship with Holly? Do you think she's right to be hesitant about getting involved with him?
3. Holly is passionate about her shop but struggles to keep it afloat. What challenges do small business owners like her face, and how does the book portray the ups and downs of entrepreneurship?
4. The novel explores the idea of perception versus reality—Caleb is seen as a Hollywood playboy, but he wants to prove to Holly that there's more to him. How does he go about changing her mind? Did you find his efforts convincing?
5. Holly fears that getting involved with Caleb will only lead to heartache. Have you ever been in a situation where you had to decide between taking a risk or playing it safe? Did you agree with Holly's initial reluctance?
6. The party Caleb hosts at The Bookish Bakery could be the turning point for Holly's struggling business. Do you think she would have succeeded without his help, or was this opportunity necessary for her growth?

7. If this book were made into a movie, what kind of atmosphere and aesthetic would you imagine for The Bookish Bakery?
8. Who would you cast as Holly and Caleb?

Author Bio

Mimi Francis is a sassy and confident romance writer known for her steamy tales of passion that leave readers breathless. Her creative writing style is filled with vivid imagery and bold characters that make her stories come alive. Born and raised in Montana, Mimi has always had a passion for writing and storytelling.

Mimi's love for writing began when she was a teenager and she honed her craft by penning countless short stories and journaling. As an adult, she turned to fan fiction as an outlet for her need to write. But it wasn't until she started writing romance novels that she truly found her niche. Her books are filled with sizzling chemistry, well-developed characters, and laugh-out-loud humor.

When she's not busy crafting her latest heartstopping romance, Mimi can be found sipping margaritas and indulging in her favorite Marvel movies. She's a self-proclaimed fangirl who can't get enough of superheroes and epic battles. But her true obsession lies with the TV show Supernatural, which she has watched from beginning to end more times than she cares to admit.

Mimi is also a wife, mother, and grandmother as well as a loving dog mom to four adorable Shih Tzus named Sebastian, Sadie, Sasha, and Sophie. Her furry companions keep her company while she writes and provide endless entertainment with their playful antics.

Mimi's writing career started with her first novel, "Private Lives," the first book in her Second Chances in Hollywood series. Since then, she has published eight more books, including the Loves of

Lakeside series, set in her home state of Montana. Mimi enjoys writing strong female leads and steamy romance scenes that leave readers wanting more.

Connect with Mimi on Instagram, Threads, and Facebook at @ author.mimi.francis, on TikTok at @authormimifrancis, or on her website mimifrancis.com.

www.ingramcontent.com/pod-product-compliance
Lightning Source LLC
Chambersburg PA
CBHW020503310726
48979CB00016B/2768/J
9798823207102